Aleksandra Osman left native Bosnia in the midst of civil war and settled in Canada. With a university degree in Comparative Literature, Aleksandra is the author of several published works that pertain to human rights.

To all the refugees and immigrants, legal aliens
of this world.

Aleksandra Osman

Story You Don't Want to Read, About People You Don't Want to Meet

Austin Macauley Publishers™
London * Cambridge * New York * Sharjah

All of the events in this memoir are true to the best of author's memory. The views expressed in this memoir are solely those of the author.

A CIP catalogue record for this title is available from the British Library.

ISBN 9781035828081 (Paperback)
ISBN 9781035828098 (ePub e-book)

www.austinmacauley.com

First Published 2024
Austin Macauley Publishers Ltd®
1 Canada Square
Canary Wharf
London
E14 5AA

Everyone has a story. We all feel that our story is the most painful, most potent, most important one. Because it's ours. As for others, we're quick to judge.

We judge by their appearance. We judge by their accent. We judge by the people they surround themselves with.

Those who genuinely suffer, who go through enormous atrocities and traumas, might become closed to the outside world but they become emphatically open to individual suffering. They can sense someone else's sincerity and pain a mile away. It's a gift, you could say.

The stories you will read are honest stories about real people, genuine facts. This is not fiction. Hopefully, once you see life through their eyes, you will look differently at anyone you might have misjudged.

My Story

It was a weekday; I was supposed to go to school. I was still asleep next to my mom, in a bedroom we shared. My grandmother opened the door and ran in, screaming, 'We're under siege! We're under siege!' I remember opening my eyes, looking at the chandelier hanging from the ceiling and then at the bright blue sky, greeting me from behind large windows covered by baroque-style curtains.

I also remember my mother's confused face as she woke up abruptly, asking my grandmother what she was talking about. I remember their quick words, the panic, the fear, the disbelief. I didn't understand what they were talking about, but I did realise it had something to do with the recent protests we had in our hometown when hundreds of thousands of people took to the streets. One thing was certain—I wouldn't be going to school on that day. 'Great!' I thought. I was supposed to have a biology quiz in school. Little did I know that day was the beginning of the end of not only my school year but my childhood.

The very beginning of the siege was not so bad, from my 11-year-old perspective.

For one, I was out of school—an unexpected spring break! Then, in between the siege and open borders for the first couple of months, many of our neighbours suddenly started moving away.

A friend of mine, who lived on the 12th floor of our building, moved to England with her family, and her grandmother gave me all of her Barbie dolls, accessories, and furniture even! I did have a few Barbies of my own, but my parents believed in extracurricular activities more than toys. So instead of buying me toys, my parents took me to ballet, music school, tennis, English classes...But now, thanks to the siege and my friend's sudden move to England—I had all the Barbie toys I never would have gotten otherwise!

Another neighbour was going to Israel with her family, and before she left, she brought us several food aid boxes from the local Jewish community centre, that included the largest selection of crushed almond chocolates that I've ever seen! And they were the tastiest ones I have ever had, to this day. Since we didn't have any other food—I could eat all the chocolate I wanted.

Also, I was suddenly allowed to wear any clothes at any time—no more formal, at home or for school categories! I could put on a special occasion dress at any time or walk around in my pyjamas at any time.

I stopped constantly being asked whether I took a shower, brushed my teeth, etc. I felt so beautifully neglected and spoiled at the same time.

Everyone around me had grim faces and spoke words silently, with fear. Sometimes, with tears too. Overnight, people we knew, and friends I used to play with in the street, were slowly disappearing from our neighbourhood. Some went abroad, some went to the other side of the trenches, some were taken down by sniper's whispers. And then, all traffic stopped. There was not a living soul on any street. Not even a stray dog. The airport was closed. Buses, trams, trains, nothing was operating.

My grandmother wasn't able to buy a fresh loaf of bread every morning; instead, she could get it only twice a week, and then, it was only once a week. They called it 'rationing'. Later, we had no food at all.

My grandma always gave me the same thing to eat during that time, for breakfast, lunch and dinner, day after day—pork fat, spread on bits of leftover bread or crackers we had at home, with sprinkles of sweet paprika and dry onion bits on it. We were collecting rain in a bucket outside on the secluded balcony—these drops of water meant the difference between life and death.

All the stores were closed. No kids were playing in the streets or on the playgrounds. No people were walking around, just an occasional car speeding by without stopping for traffic lights. The phones weren't working, there was no electricity or water. I didn't understand why it was all like that, but I did understand that something horrible was happening. Something important, something that made people sad and afraid. Worst of all, it made them dead.

One day, I entered our living room to find everyone in the room crying: my mom, grandmother, grandfather and my older uncle. I asked what happened, but no one could say anything…my mom just said something that sounded like 'Nina…' and continued crying.

Nina

Her name was Nina. She was 10 years old, one year junior to me. I remember seeing her for the last time on a beach near the small town of Ston, close to Dubrovnik, in August of 1990, the town where both our families spent summers. She was such a stunning beauty, even at that tender age—everyone looked at her wherever she went. She had long blond hair that slightly curled at the ends, large blue eyes, and a smile that could melt the Snow Queen's heart.

But what captured everyone the most, I believe, were her posture and that sense of grace. She was a child, but she was a well-composed child, confident and intelligent. You could tell that just by looking at her walk or listening to her speak, she always seemed so much more mature than any of her peers.

We talked for a little while that last time I saw her. September was just around the corner. We were both going back to our hometown of Sarajevo where we lived and went to school. She was showing me a straw hat she bought that year from street vendors during one of the traditional festivals on the Croatian coast. I was showing her my neon yellow tights, a fashion must-have of that year. To this day, I can clearly see her standing opposite me, in a white one-piece bathing suit with that straw hat on her head, smiling. We talked about our schools, about our families. I was about to get a baby sister, and she had a baby brother, so we were sharing our experiences and expectations. Our families were friends, so we ended the conversation with 'see you soon in Sarajevo.'

Her mother was a pharmacist, a beautiful dark-haired lady, so much like Sophia Loren. Older people always referred to her as a 'Mediterranean beauty'. She was a native of the small town we spent summers in. In that town, she met her husband, Nina's father, fell in love with him and then moved to his hometown of Sarajevo, where they started a family.

Nina's father was an engineer, a quiet, good-hearted man who loved his family more than anything in the world. What I remember about him the most is his kindness, ever-present smile and the thick prescription glasses he wore. And the moustache. He was not the macho type of man one would usually imagine seeing by someone as beautiful as Nina's mom. But he was her king. And his daughter Nina—she was the apple of his eye.

I remember visiting them once with my parents. Nina always had the newest toys… all the toys you could imagine…she had the first neon markers, the coolest item of our generation that year. I also remember one shameful moment when I couldn't resist wanting to have one of those neon markers myself. So, before leaving home, I slipped a yellow one into my pocket, but then I saw a purple one too and the neon blue one as well. I had to have them all! I'll never forget the bitter conscience I felt the second I put the markers into my pocket!

Of course, I happened to have a hole in my pocket, and as we were saying goodbye in the hallway, all of the markers suddenly started falling out of my pocket. And there they were, right on the floor beside my feet, right before we left, for everyone to see. Everyone looked at me and my face turned red like never before—or after, in my life. My mom was embarrassed, Nina's parents were smiling but Nina just picked up the markers off the floor, took them to her room and came back to say bye as if nothing had happened. Even that last time I saw her, on the beach, the first time after the 'marker incident', she behaved as if nothing had happened. That's the way she was. She already knew how to disarm and empower her peers at the same time, at that very young age.

When the war started, I didn't think of her much. She lived in a different neighbourhood and we didn't see each other all that often, once school had started. But now, I saw my mom's right hand go over her mouth, I heard her whisper 'no', I saw tears in her eyes. I walked into the living room to ask what they were talking about—I knew I heard Nina's name.

They told me that Nina was in a hospital, she was injured by a grenade shrapnel the size of a peppercorn. My older uncle, an orthopaedic surgeon, head of the Emergency Department, was working the previous evening when more innocent victims of artillery fire were brought in. Nina was among them.

My uncle had tears in his eyes. He was telling my mom that that was one of the worst moments of his career, of his life. He was doing trauma work for over two decades but that moment when he saw Nina's father rush into the ER with Nina, was inexplicably difficult. Her father carried her lifeless bloody body and on seeing my uncle, he pierced the air with his screams, 'Save her, please save her!'

My uncle did all he could, and other doctors did too, but the tiny piece of shrapnel went straight into her brain, right in the middle of her head and she was comatose from the beginning. It was completely inoperable; she could not be saved. It just couldn't be taken out. She just could not be saved. She was already dead. Her father was inconsolable, he was sobbing, screaming with pain, and collapsing on the floor. She was the apple of his eye and now she was dead.

'Unfathomable,' my uncle was saying. Of all the places and all the possible scenarios, this had to be the scenario that was written for her—her destiny. She wasn't even out in the open where a sniper could easily aim at her; she wasn't at a large gathering queuing with a canister to get water or foreign food aid. She was right in front of her building, some 3 metres in front of the building lobby, sheltered by that 7-storey building on one side, other buildings to the left and right, and high trees that sheltered her from the sky. She was playing with other kids from the building…she was supposed to be safe. As safe as possible. But they threw a grenade from the hills, aiming for a bridge some 700 metres away, behind a block of other buildings.

Of course, shrapnel flew everywhere, but a very tiny one somehow flew so far that it hit her. And just like that, her life ended. Just like that, her parents lost the only daughter they had; her brother lost a sister he'd never remember. Just like that, because 'someone' up in the hills surrounding Sarajevo, simply decided to play God, to throw a grenade on civilians. Just like that. No reason at all. As if any reason would justify it. My uncle was very shaken, and so was my mother. This was their friends' daughter in question. My friend. And she died. My uncle couldn't save her. No one could.

A part of her parents died that day as well, a large part of them. Her brother was still too small to understand much, but for her parents, this was the end of the world. Nina's mother has always been the stronger one in the family, the rational one, but for a long time to come, she couldn't rationalise the fact that her daughter died. She faded on the inside, aged rapidly on the outside, and barely kept herself sane. Every time she passed by Nina's room, she sobbed. Every time she closed her eyes, she sobbed. Every time she opened her eyes, she sobbed.

Nina was everywhere around her, and nowhere around her. Yet she was present as if she never left. But she was so far away, never to return. She would never hold her daughter again, she could never kiss her daughter again, and she would never comb her long blond hair. She would never hear about her heartaches, she would never see her little girl grow up, walk down the aisle, or become a mother. All that was taken away from her. Why? What on Earth did she ever do to anyone? Why?

Nina's father was broken, completely broken down that day. Nina was his life and now she was gone. From that day on, he didn't care where he was walking and when he was going out. He didn't care much if he died. He continued living, though. He did know that his wife and his son needed him, but he had no strength. He was vegetating. His soul couldn't take it. Within weeks of Nina's death, he suddenly lost his sight. He always had strong prescription and eyesight problems, but this blindness came much too suddenly.

Doctors said that it was known to happen in highly stressful situations, when people went through a great shock and as a reaction to it, they would lose sight. They were right, that was his story. Although completely blind, he could still clearly see his Nina's smiling face and open arms running to him for a hug. But she was gone, he knew that.

His wife, Nina's mother, suddenly had not only a dead daughter to grieve for, but a blind husband to take care of and a young son to raise, in a war-ravaged, occupied city. She was not the only one with a story, but this was her life, her story, her very own loss, her very own scar. Not everyone lost their dearest ones in this senseless war, but she did. Still, every time she looked into her young son's eyes and saw him smile, although he was hungry, dirty, and thirsty, she smiled. And she saw why she had to go on. She gathered all the strength she could, knowing she had no choice. Even when her husband suddenly died a few months later, she knew she had to go on.

He died of a broken heart, in the rare moments of ceasefire when everything was calm… for a few moments, at least. He was sitting on the floor with his eyes open and simply stopped living. The truth is—he died months before, along with Nina. His wife knew that. He was just an apparition, walking around, hardly speaking, hardly breathing, silent while tears were falling from his frozen eyes. His heart was numbed a long time ago.

Nina's mother had stayed completely alone in the world with her little son. Her husband was buried, in a grave…one grave, among thousands of graves in what once used to be a soccer stadium. There was no ceremony; there was no time for tears, for speeches, for goodbyes. There was hardly any space left for more victims. He was buried and that was it. Like everyone else, Nina's mom had to continue living. For a long, long time, she tried to pretend that both her husband and her daughter had simply gone away on a trip, a very, very long trip…but that they were well. And she stayed in Sarajevo with her son, living through the artillery philharmonic orchestra the best way she knew how just as everyone else did.

So, she'd take her son's hand and go into the shelter every time the siren sounded. Like everyone else, she'd go to get water from the mobile cistern, her son in one hand, a plastic jug in the other. Like everyone else, she went to the UNPROFOR truck to get food aid. Like everyone else, she continued living, although most of her being had died. She had no choice—her son only had her. She poured all the tears out of her eyes until she had none. She had dried out.

She survived the war. So did her son. They were half dead by the time it all ended; numb in spirit, numb in body, but alive. They still had their brains intact, both arms, both legs attached, both eyes, and both ears. They were a few of the lucky ones. Ironically. The first opportunity she had, she packed the little she had left, the little that she needed, and moved with her son to her tiny hometown on the coast. Her son started going to school there, playing with other kids and learning the meaning of the term 'being alive'. She started working as a pharmacist again, and one could say that life continued as normal as possible for her.

But every evening, and especially in early dawns, she would become an apparition sitting on a bench by the sea, lifelessly looking at the waves. Sometimes for a few minutes, sometimes for several hours. At home, sometimes she'd change channels if there was a little blonde girl on TV.

Sometimes she'd get teary-eyed if she saw a father walking with his daughter on the street. But that was her life. A life of never-ending, suppressed sorrow, a life of bitter-sweet memories, a life too short and too long at the same time. But if was her life. And she had to learn to be grateful to be able to live it.

That's what we in Sarajevo, did too. Perhaps we were all at enormous risk, likelihood even, of dying at any given moment, but we weren't dead yet. And we did have to breathe on, live on, through and with the circumstances we were in.

Right before the war started, my family and I lived in an old communist building, right across the street from an enclosed military base. I remember looking through our kitchen window one day, observing the convoy of military tanks and trucks leaving the base. The siege soon turned into a heavy artillery symphony, heartened by snipers and bomber fireworks. Several floors of the building we lived in were burned.

One day, a grenade fell into my sister's crib, just a few minutes after my mom took her out of it and went into the living room with her. They both survived, but my mother had several shrapnel pieces stuck in her legs. On that day, they were very lucky, as the grenade exploded on the roof, before falling into my sister's crib. Had it exploded just a few seconds later, I'd be an orphan without any siblings today.

We were such easy targets… all of us, in Sarajevo. Surrounded by hills and mountains all of which were occupied by enemy soldiers to whom we must have looked like a buffet of human crawlers…which of us would they choose to kill first?

The building where my younger uncle lived was slightly better shielded and safer than the buildings the rest of the family lived in. So, everyone moved to my uncle's 2-bedroom apartment in a different area of the city. When I say 'moved', I'm not talking about a big U-Haul truck with boxes. By 'move', I mean running to a car filled in with some not clearly identifiable mixture of plain sunflower oil, gas residue and water—hoping that it will not fail us. Then we drove that car as fast as possible through back alleys, while buildings provided a peek-a-boo shield from snipers, hoping we wouldn't die.

While driving through an open space, when there was no other choice, sniper hits would dance around our car…I was lying in the back, not seat, but foot area. There were tears and silent screams in the car. Thankfully, we did arrive, alive. That's how we moved to my uncle's apartment. With nothing in our hands except for a tiny bag with a few items belonging to my baby sister.

I have this strong visual, to this day, 30 years later, of my mom carrying my baby sister who was dressed in a red, quilted two-piece with a brown teddy bear applique on top. My mother was crying, my sister blissfully sucking on a rubber teether toy, completely unaware of anything happening around her.

My uncle's wife and child left for Portugal, but my uncle wasn't allowed to leave as he was a doctor. My mother wasn't allowed to leave either, for the same reason, or my other uncle or his wife. If you were a doctor, you weren't allowed to leave under any conditions. If you were a male of legal age, you also weren't allowed to leave as you would be recruited to fight. Most volunteered for the army anyhow, we simply had no one to defend us but ourselves. At least initially when it was the most crucial for us to get help.

My uncle lived in a residential area famous for its upper and lower rows of red brick townhouses and condos that sheltered narrow streets flowing through the area. The upside was that we kids, who lived there, could meet in front of townhouse entrances and hang out. No one from the hills could see us, or shoot at us. It gave us a temporary feeling of normalcy amid very abnormal circumstances.

My uncle and aunt always had the best food; my aunt always had the best clothes too. I remember opening her closet and trying out the clothes and jewellery she left behind. She had sequin dresses and high heels! Something my mom never wore or owned. I also remember us opening their freezer and seeing bags and bags of frozen berries, cherries, broccoli, and mixed veggies—all defrosted and occupied by white maggots. Scarce to non-existent electricity supply did its magic.

The national defence army, consisting of recruits and volunteers, had its headquarters near my uncle's apartment. The water cistern would occasionally arrive and either I or someone else from my family would go out with a canister and queue up to get the only drinking water we had access to. At times when artillery fire was raging and it was too dangerous to get drinking water, we'd use rainwater that my grandmother gathered in a large plastic container on my uncle's balcony.

Soon, people with blue helmets started showing up in the neighbourhood. They spoke English and French, but not our language…and they had letters 'U N P R O F O R' written on their helmets. They were very nice to everybody, and we kids loved speaking with them and showing off our foreign language skills.

Those skills mostly consisted of New Kids on the Block, George Michael and U2 songs vocabulary. Once there were these journalists, asking questions and everyone around us was talking about getting an intervention, so when they approached me, I enthusiastically said 'We need an intervention, urgently! Tell the US we need an intervention.' I didn't understand what I was talking about at all, I just wanted to show off my English-speaking skills. Had I understood those words then, I would have not only spoken but screamed them with passion and conviction much, much earlier, before so many innocent people lost their lives.

Yes, most of these international soldiers were nice, but not nearly as nice as our local soldiers.

There was an empty office space on the ground floor of my uncle's condo building, where our soldiers would receive foreign aid and distribute it to us, the locals. We were very, very hungry and were, naturally, looking forward to eating anything. However, the food aid we received was very strange—it was all packed in aluminium sachets like shampoo samples and labelled with strange names such as 'Yorkshire pudding', 'Tabasco', and so on. That was the first time I tried peanut butter and ate pork mixed with apple sauce.

This was not the type of food I was used to. No one in my country was. None of us had ever heard of Tabasco, and I still remember the swears once, starved as we were, a neighbour hungrily gulped the sauce down, not realising it was spicy. Why on Earth would anyone think of sending Tabasco as food aid to starving people? It is still a mystery to me. Milk powder was good though, my mother mixed it with rainwater so she could feed my baby sister.

The food aid we were being sent had some very odd meals. More often than not, we had no option but to pick dandelion leaves and eat them raw, as veggies. We also gathered trefoils, pulled out one by one purple spike and sucked their bottom—it sounds disgusting, but it tasted like sugar. That was our chocolate, ice cream and cake all in one. War dessert.

My mother once cooked everyone semolina that she found in my uncle's kitchen. I noticed tiny white worms in it and told everyone. They all looked in their plates and simply said they had them too, without any fuss at all. My mother just waved her hand in the air and continued eating. So did my grandmother, my uncle, and my grandfather. I wasn't hungry anymore, and my baby sister had no idea what she was eating anyhow.

When the artillery fire was getting stronger and stronger, we'd run to the underground bunker refuge, built in the WW1 period. It was right next to my uncle's building but getting there was not that simple—there were a few metres of unobstructed view from the hills diving us from the safe refuge. Those few metres were like walking on a death rope.

Some would cross to the other side, some would fall. We'd run so fast over that clear area, like a bunny taking a large leap, and falling onto the underground stairs leading into the refuge. The refuge was all grey. And cold. And huge. There were many people in the underground bunker, gathered in little groups. We all chatted quietly as if someone out there could hear us, only occasionally our chat would be silenced by the deafening sound of a grenade explosion nearby, or a crying baby.

The people in blue helmets arranged a new ceasefire agreement with the enemy, to facilitate a convoy of mothers and children. It would be the last convoy allowed to leave the city, but it would still be a very risky trip to freedom as the convoy had to go through the enemy territory in order to leave the city.

In the past, one of those convoys was bombarded, despite a previous ceasefire agreement, and hundreds of mothers and children died.

My sister was still a baby, so my mother—although a doctor, was given permission to leave. My mom was afraid but said it was better to try to leave than it was to stay. My baby sister was a preemie, and if anything were to happen or if she ended up needing hospital care or specific medication, it was unlikely she'd be able to get it. My mom was afraid of that too. So, she decided that she would leave, with me and my baby sister.

My mom had no savings, like most people her age today. Those were different times. I remember her asking my grandmother for money so that she has something with her while trying to leave the city. My grandma was reluctant in parting with it—her money, that is, not us.

My grandmother always had money, lots of it. Once I surprised her when she was in our study, and I saw her put down a mattress under which there was a pile of paper bills. A pile, literally. I recall thinking how cool that was, like in cartoons! You know when Donald Duck gets into a bathtub full of green bills? This was something like that, but under the mattress.

Once my grandma noticed I was standing there, I got into a lot of trouble. Yes, my grandma always had money, but when my mom asked her for it, she refused, telling my mom that she simply couldn't spare any money, in uncertain times. My mother yelled at her for being so selfish and insensitive. She was leaving the city with two small children, me and my sister, without a penny in her pocket, not knowing if she'll arrive alive and grandma wouldn't help her in a situation like that? My grandma replied that she didn't understand why my mom was leaving with us at all.

'If we need to die, we should die together,' my grandma said. My mother, grandfather and uncle were shocked. After a cacophonic verbal exchange, my grandma agreed to give my mother one thousand Deutsch marks (the only trusted foreign currency at that time), but only if she could sell my mom's car to get that money back. My mom was crying, my uncle was screaming, my grandfather was against it too, but grandma wouldn't budge. So, my mom agreed, with a heavy heart.

Thinking about it, my grandma has always been like that. She liked money more than anything. When I was 10, I got some money for a birthday from my relatives, so I wanted to use it to throw a birthday party and invite a few friends over. My grandma reluctantly agreed, but only if I gave her all my birthday money, as she said she didn't have enough money to make me a cake *and* buy snacks. She said she'd use her money to buy ingredients for the cake, but I had to give her all my birthday money to buy snacks, juice, etc.

I knew she wasn't telling the truth, but I gave her all my birthday money just so I could have my first very own birthday party. I was allowed to invite 3 friends to my first birthday 'party'. No balloons, no confetti, no thematic paper plates or napkins, but we did have some pickles, pepperoni sausage, bread, pretzels and my grandma's classic—walnut birthday cake. Yes, my grandma has always been a bit different. After that, I'd always hide any money I'd ever get—or find—under my bedroom carpet, and I'd never tell her about it.

Anyhow, grandma gave my mom the money so that we can leave with the convoy. My mom took one tiny bag and we filled it as much as we could with my aunt's clothes—we had none of our own, they were left in our apartment in a different area of the city. My mom also took a little backpack with my sister's blankie and a few toys, as well as cloth diapers. It would be short-term, we thought. We'd be back soon in Sarajevo, we thought. This nonsense of war would all stop before winter, and we'd come back to celebrate all the winter holidays with all of our friends. So, we thought.

I remember talking about it with my grandfather while sorting rosehips on my uncle's sheltered balcony. My grandpa found a rosehip that was shaped like a backside and showed it to me. The laughter we shared that moment was the most beautiful, happiest emotion I recall, throughout those 7 months spent in the besieged city.

The day we left the city was the last time I saw my grandfather alive. He was standing on that same balcony with tears in his eyes, beaming a big smile and waving us goodbye. I knew that that was the last time I'd ever see him, so I made effort to create a mental picture, and take a mental snapshot. To this day, the recollection of that memory still makes me cry.

We left the city on Friday, 13 November 1992, having spent 7 months in the war. My grandfather died of metastasised cancer, a week later, on 21 November. The Dayton agreement, officially ending the war, was signed in 1995. War ended, but scars never will.

A week after we arrived to Croatia, my uncle also managed to leave the city in order to reunite with his wife and son. We saw him briefly in Zagreb before he went to Portugal. It took us 27 years to meet again in person. My stepdad joined us in Croatia after a year. Throughout our stay in Zagreb, my mom was working either only short-term or freelance. My stepdad even less. I was attending the local elementary school and was made fun of because of my dialect, because of my lack of knowledge of the material they were working on, because I wore clothes that were too big, and too old-fashion.

Because I ate a lot. It was futile to even try to explain to them that while they were learning that material in school—I was in an underground shelter. While they were throwing eggs for fun—I spent the year dreaming of tasting one. My dialect was different as I was from a different place but lacking knowledge of their jargon didn't mean that I lacked intelligence.

My clothes were the way they were because it was all we were able to grab—I had just turned 12 at the time and the clothes mostly belonged to my aunt. And yes, I was poor at that time. I had no money for chewing gum, pastry, or drinks. None of it. We were scrambling just to make ends meet. That period of poverty, being a legal alien, a refugee, often felt worse than those months spent in a besieged city.

The kids can be very cruel, you know…adults as well. There were only four kids in the entire school who took me as their equal, defended me and guided me. Only four. As a refugee, I was an easy target, but even after we obtained full residency status, I was never accepted as one of them. I never assimilated. Eventually, I didn't want to, either.

Seeing that the war would not end, and we had no money left at all, my parents applied for immigration status in several countries abroad. One of them accepted us—Canada. Ironically, we were leaving for a new, completely foreign country, hoping to continue living our old lives. To pick up the pieces of life we had left and build a new foundation on them…the one that would provide stability and security for my parents, my sister and myself. To continue where we left off.

That wasn't the case, though. Along the way, we met many people from different walks of life, different cultures, all united in common pain…or better, common pain points. Through their eyes, and eventually our own, we saw many things differently than expected. We learned that grass is definitely not greener on the other side. If it is, it is scentless. We learned never to judge anyone, by their cover or by any single one of their pages, as they all have a story woven of many fonts. We learned that insisting on tolerance is the very opposite of tolerance itself. We learned that diversity and multiculturalism don't necessarily strengthen our individuality but can also weaken it.

We learned that theory and practice are not the same. We also learned that there is a very, very thin line between democracy and anarchy. We learned that by having more, one is left with less. We learned that sometimes, taking a few steps back will get you faster to your goal ahead. And we realised that the best times we had are behind us, not ahead of us. And sometimes, but only sometimes—that was not the case.

I got asked several times in Canada, our new home, whether we had washrooms back in my homeland…whether we had TVs. At first, I thought those were jokes and laughed them off. Upon realising they were very sincere; I would be overcome with immense sadness and shame…ignorance is not always bliss. Now I see that what I should have felt, is a pity that they just didn't know any better. Pity that their general knowledge was so lacking, so limited.

I recall a situation upon our arrival to Canada. The ethereally beautiful blinking lights of the city we admired from the airplane, were replaced by the blinking eyes of my mother, whose tears were landing down her face upon our arrival to the so-called 'Welcome House'—an immigrant gathering centre, where we were provided with initial accommodation.

Promised Land

'You've got to be kidding!' My mother said through tears, hardly believing her eyes. She was looking at two illustrations, taped to the wall of the Welcome House washroom. Both showed an image of a person and a toilet seat. The upper image showed a person standing on the toilet seat with both feet, and with their knees bent. It was crossed out, implying it is the wrong way to use the toilet. The other image showed a person properly sitting on the toilet seat and had a green checkmark next to it, implying that this was the correct way to use the toilet. These illustrations were so shockingly simplistic and so utterly profound at the same time, pointing to the obvious diversity of the newcomers' backgrounds.

My mother realised that she had just become yet another newcomer, in Canada's eyes.

Did she have to leave her homeland? No, not exactly. The war was officially over. But she felt like she needed to leave her homeland…for all our sakes. The wounds of war were still fresh and omnipresent. She wasn't sure if she'd get her old job back…the buildings, schools and hospitals were still damaged and there was extensive reconstruction to be done…not just on architecture but on every aspect of life there.

She expected Canada to be different… but just how different—she wasn't prepared for that. She was an ophthalmologist, an eye surgeon, with over 25 years of experience. She worked as a member of the international medical team when her homeland hosted the Winter Olympic Games in 1984. She travelled extensively throughout Europe, played piano, and spoke 4 languages fluently.

In some better, pre-war times, she would spend summers in her family's vacation home on the Adriatic Coast and winters were spent in the family's other vacation home, in the enchanting mountains of Jahorina. She grew up in an eminent surgeon family, having surgeon siblings, cousins even.

None of that mattered, not anymore, as the washroom illustration clearly alluded. She was now just a number, just one of the countless faceless people labelled as newcomers who may or may not know how to use a toilet. Still, after the initial shock, my mother decided to believe that the illustration was just that—an illustration, and that each newcomer must have been judged individually, based on their individual merit. Oh, how wrong she was!

Once a newcomer, always a newcomer. Regardless of whether your family arrived 4 generations ago, or if you arrived 2 days ago—you were never a fully deserving Canadian citizen. They would never allow it. It was always under the mask of multiculturalism, acceptance, and tolerance but in fact, they didn't want you to belong *only* to Canada. They always reminded you of your background, as if to remind you to know your place. Not to help you fit in; rather, to make sure you never belong.

My mother truly was from a liberal, multicultural family. A Jew, a Muslim, a Catholic and an Orthodox enter the room…and it's not a joke. It was all our family, at a family gathering. She was genuinely open to all religions, languages, and cultures.

But Canada's diversity was not the standard kind. It was set up in such a way that no one felt respected; it was a melange of clashing spices. The result was a potluck that was very diverse, but inedible. She realised it immediately upon arrival.

In such a diverse country, she was the only genuine minority. Her skin colour, her beliefs, and even her outfits. She was very self-conscious of her thick English accent until she realised that the manager of the Welcome House, in an English-speaking country, managed the entire hotel-size facility—with absolutely none, whatsoever knowledge of any English at all.

The very first day she arrived to Canada, in early March, my mother put on her raincoat, leather knee high boots and went for a walk around the block with my stepdad. It was a casual outfit she'd throw on back home, but in Canada, she was overdressed.

She expected she'd obtain a job soon. 'Ha! Mrs. Doctor, grab a mop if you want to feed your family!' One of her acquaintances said. My mother was genuinely surprised and saddened by that sentence. Her acquaintance came to Canada from the same homeland, but many years earlier. She was experienced in the ways of this new country. That is what made this advice so much more terrifying. It hung in the back of my mother's mind, sometimes as a motivating reminder, other times as a depressant.

Employment in her profession was not easy to find, indeed. She could easily work as a salesperson at a fast-food restaurant or a salesperson at a retail store. But why would she do that? It was not what she was skilled at, it was not what she was educated for. She was raised with belief that everyone had their own skills, that everyone chooses their own calling, and then works and studies towards it. Medicine was hers.

So why could she not continue to do so in her new home, in Canada? Wasn't the acceptance and respect of individuals the very definition of multiculturalism, be it their religion, race, background, or education? Why was she then disrespected by not being allowed to work in her profession? Was she not an asset to Canada? She was already educated, skilled, and experienced in that field.

Despite resistance, she realised that there was no choice but to go on social assistance. That too, was not an easy feat. Ironically, my mother was not allowed to work in her profession but going on social assistance was just as an intimidating task.

'Have you looked for a job recently?' The income assistance officer asked.

'Yes, many times,' she replied with a thick accent in stuttering English, intimidated by the question's matter-of-factness.

'Do you have copies of the applications?' The officer continued.

'Yes, at home. I applied to hospitals, clinics, universities…' She struggled to continue her sentence, but the officer interrupted.

'Sorry, what kind of jobs did you apply for?' The officer laughed, casually breezing through my mother's file.

'I am a doctor,' she replied.

'Oh…' the officer smirked, 'You know you won't be able to find a job as a doctor, right? But, if you like medicine, you can try to find some other hospital staff positions that are non-union, perhaps cleaning staff at a hospital, or some sort of other hospital help to start with?'

She looked at the officer with tears in her eyes, not being sure whether it was a joke.

'But I am a doctor, I am sorry, I don't understand…' she tried to reason with the officer.

'I know Mme, you're a doctor. Ok. Good for you. But you can't work as a doctor. Do you understand me?' the officer looked at her, as if my mother didn't understand English.

'I understand you, but I can't believe it. I am a doctor; you want me to find a job cleaning?' she asked on the verge of panic.

'I don't appreciate you raising your voice at me Mme!' The officer raised her voice.

'I am not…' she tried to reply but was interrupted.

'You did Mme, and I don't appreciate it! You cannot work as a doctor. You will have to find other jobs if you want to feed your family!'

She started crying, while the officer sat behind a computer and started typing.

'How do you pronounce your name Mme? Ya-drunk-a?' The officer said, trying to keep a straight face.

My mother started crying hearing her name butchered. She was named after the clear blue Adriatic Sea; one this officer probably never heard of or had any interest in finding out about. After all, my mother was just another newcomer asking for social assistance. Yet another nameless face, as all names were unpronounceable, and all faces forgettable. Why would you need the names and faces when they were given numbers?

'Don't cry. Don't cry Mme. You need to find a job; do you understand me? I will register you for social assistance, but you need to bring me copies of the job applications you sent, and you need to come back every month with copies of job applications to continue to have social assistance. If you find a job, you need to let us know immediately and then we take you off social assistance. Do you understand?'

She was stunned. Frozen. She felt naked, alone, helpless, speechless.

'Yes, she does,' I replied on her behalf.

It was clear that she was nudged into a direction she didn't want, a direction she didn't expect to be pushed into. *Had she known that both her and her husband would be expected to take a no-skill, low-income job in order just to put food on the table, she would have stayed in her Bosnia, Croatia...anywhere but here.* She paused, realising the potency of her thought.

That moment was the beginning of her end; a long, dark path leading to the abyss.

So far, Welcome House was everything but welcoming, and Canada's idea of multiculturalism and democracy seemed closer to anarchy.

My sister and I, however, seemed to have adapted well. We had friends, albeit also newcomers from the same homeland. We picked up the local accent immediately.

I started working at the age of 15, despite protests from my family back home. You see, in my homeland minors are not expected to concentrate on anything except education until they complete university studies—which everyone does. In fact, it is illegal to work until you reach legal age and are out of school! It was very difficult to convince my mother of all the benefits of my getting a job—and adding to the family income. But I did it.

In the meantime, my mother struggled with the fact that from being a doctor at a hospital, she went to a no-name apparition, accountable to the non-English speaking staff at an anglophone social welfare office.

Every month, she would take a 3-cm thick pile of application forms to her social assistance officer, to prove that she was indeed looking for a job. And every month, that same officer, would speak in a degrading manner, asking her to lower her job criteria even lower. Or that's what it came across as. My mother might have misunderstood it, however, as the officer also spoke with a very thick accent, in almost incomprehensible English.

Months turned into years, but eventually, she did obtain a job as a technician in an ophthalmologist's office, perplexing her social assistance officer with her 'success'. Was it a triumph? No. She spent over 10 years just educating herself to perform surgeries on people's eyes, worked another 25 years doing exactly that and now she was clicking buttons on a machine that did the prescription measurements for her, before automatically sending them off to the practising ophthalmologist. No, it was not a success. Albeit, considering she did not, after all, have to 'grab a mop to survive'—you could consider it a success.

It didn't last long, though. My mother was like a salmon in a pool of piranhas that belonged to a different cultural ghetto. These piranhas worked the same job as she did, but were enjoying the fact that unlike them, unskilled labourers, my mother used to be an ophthalmologist. You see, these piranhas could have obtained any education they wanted in their own homeland—had they been willing to study for it. Instead, they did other things, and upon arriving to Canada, they just got the fastest certificate that would enable them to work an office job closest to the field of medicine.

So, they were thrilled with the fact that they, with little effort, were doing the same job as someone who actually put an enormous amount of effort in her own education. Not only did they have fun with my mother, but they also became downright bullies. You know the little things that intimidate you, tiny daily doses of backstabbing and mobbing that are present in just the right amount to hurt you, but not enough to report? Those chronic doses of viciousness. But she endured it for as much as she could with help of whatever she could.

Sometimes, it was an anti-depressant before going to bed. Sometimes, it was trying to simply ignore them. My mother knew we needed her to work, we needed to pay bills, buy food. My job was not enough to help put food on the table. My stepdad could not get a job anywhere as his knowledge of English was quite poor, despite all the language courses he was taking. No wonder—most of those courses were taught by non-English speakers to start with. And social assistance office only looked at 'family income' when considering whether to provide assistance, or not.

It didn't matter that one of my parents was unemployed, that there were us, kids, in the family. So, my mother held onto the job during the day, smiling at patients and every night she would put a sedative under her tongue, numbing her heart and soul before drifting away to dreamland. Until she just couldn't anymore.

My mother knew that she could never be happy in Canada. She felt raped by its false promises and pretences. She was disappointed with herself for not being patient with her homeland, for not giving it enough time to heal. She felt like a child who was bribed by a magical forest that turned out to be nothing more than a moving background, a photo prop.

She borrowed money from my uncle and bought a one-way ticket for us all, to go back to our homeland. Would it be perfect? No. But this was quite imperfect as well. However, unlike Canada, her homeland never gave her false promises. Her homeland awaited her, raw in all its imperfection, but it awaited her with open arms and warm familiarity.

Sitting on the airplane flying back to her homeland, she admiringly watched the dark lights of the city she was leaving. It looked so beautiful and glistening. But she knew, not all that shines is gold.

Hers was not the only lesson to be learned. And she was not the only one to have learned a lesson. While living in Canada, we met many people from our region, a region called the Balkans. As soon as we'd leave our respectful countries, we would be grouped abroad…grouped as a blob called the Balkans, united in sadness over our destiny and anger over being unappreciated, reduced to a number, reduced to the lowest skill possible.

The adults from the Balkans, who came to Canada the same way and at the same time we did, had a hard time coping with it. They were often offered sedatives and sleeping pills by health professionals to help them cope with it all. Instead, the families took turns hosting family gatherings, where they would eat, talk, laugh. I remember one time when my parents hosted it. My mom made our traditional minced meat pie, we had snacks, wine and of course—Turkish coffee, which they'd drink sometimes at 10 pm.

I remember the wonderful cacophony of laughter, the words spoken, the sounds of music from our region travelling through the air. They'd share stories and tips and reminisce about the life they all had to leave behind. And each one of those families had a story of its own, similar to ours.

Our rental building was full of immigrants, many from the Balkans, but from other European areas as well. All of them had children. There was a couple that my parents met in the most awkward way. While waiting for the elevator in our rental building, a couple with a small boy entered the lobby and told the boy whose name was Vladi: 'Vladi, fuck.' The boy went to the elevator's 'down' button and pressed it.

My parents looked at each other, almost bursting out in laughter, my mother quietly asking my stepdad whether he heard the same. Thinking they didn't understand properly, they continued quietly waiting for the elevator to arrive.

The couple then repeated: 'Vladi, fuck.' And the boy pressed the same elevator button again. At this point, my mother couldn't hold it anymore and she burst out laughing, covering her mouth out of embarrassment. My father soon started to laugh as well. The boy's parents, realising what was happening, started laughing and approached my parents, explaining that they spoke Romanian and that in Romanian word 'fak', pronounced as 'fuck', means 'to push the button'. It was a crazy way to meet someone, but on that day, they started a friendship that lasts to this day.

However, there is a memory of another couple that brings tears to my eyes—and their stay in Canada is a memory they'd rather not have.

Anonymous Complaint

Amra and Stefan were like most immigrants—normal, educated people who were forced by circumstances to look for refuge in Canada. Initially, they were catapulted by war from their native war-ravaged town of Sarajevo to Greece, where they lived for a few years as refugees. Contrary to popular presumptions of bad refugee shelter conditions, refugee conditions in Greece were quite excellent at that time. Both of them had full medical coverage, very decent financial social assistance and were able to rent a beautiful apartment. Stefan was an academic painter, and so was Amra. When she got pregnant, she completely dedicated her time to preparations for the baby, while he spent his time in the streets, painting face portraits of tourists and making quite a bit of money doing it!

After all, they had a baby on the way and wanted to do all they could to secure a good future for their child. They hoped to provide a better kind of life so that their son wouldn't have to worry if he'd be surprised by war, if he'd get out of it alive, if he'd have enough money to start anew. Because life doesn't give you guarantees.

When their son was born, they were in their third year of refuge in Greece and although Greece and Greeks treated them exceptionally, there was always that uncertainty in the air—what if Greece suddenly cut their refugee status, what if they could never get the Greek citizenship, what if the war continued raging and they couldn't get back to Sarajevo for years to come, what if, what if...Therefore, they thought it'd be best for them and their son's future to go overseas and look for certainty there. Not just to start anew but also to finally drop the anchor somewhere.

After all, they had to think of their son and any future children they wanted to have. Once you have children, you had to settle down, you had to have a base. The decision was made. They sold the few things they bought in 3 years of their stay in Greece, packed their suitcases and arrived to Canada with their child.

It wasn't easy, but considering it wasn't the first time they were starting from scratch, it wasn't difficult either. They settled down, received immigration papers, started receiving social assistance and after 5 years spent in the country, they would be eligible to obtain citizenship.

The conditions were all black on white and the couple was happy that they finally had something definite and defined in their hands, something they could count on. Amra wasn't working—she was taking care of their son. As for Stefan, it took him some time to find a job, but he did—delivering pizzas, mostly working night shifts. This was a far cry from his profession, but he didn't complain. All the newcomers had to pass the same route, go through the same experiences. You start at the very bottom and build your life up, isn't that so?

Amra got pregnant again soon and 3 years after their arrival to Canada, their then 4-year-old son got a baby brother. Although he was happy to have someone he could play with, the boy didn't like the fact that he wasn't the centre of attention anymore. He didn't like the fact that he had to share the attention with that little cooing bundle. Like most children in that situation, he was becoming jealous. Parents did their best not to make him feel neglected, but in some situations, the small baby simply required more attention. She was alone with the children most of the time, with no help from anyone, so she did the best she could.

To become the centre of attention again, the older son would sometimes come to get a hug, sometimes he would pretend to be crying, sometimes he would be loud, angry or he'd even scream. Throwing tantrums became a daily routine for him. As the parents knew why he was doing this, they forgave and ignored this behaviour, as recommended by their family doctor. They waited for it to pass. It was not an easy task.

One Saturday, Amra finally managed to put to sleep the 7-month-old son and started making lunch, while her husband Stefan was finally able to get some rest, having spent the entire night delivering pizzas. Their older son decided to take advantage of his brother being asleep to try to get all the attention for himself. First, he started meddling in the kitchen, being around his mother's feet and she had to tell him to move away because the stove was on. She couldn't give him all her attention and cook lunch at the same time.

The boy then went to his father who was sleeping on the couch and jumped on his stomach with all his strength, thinking father would find it funny. Suddenly awoken and in stomach pain, his father raised his voice, put the son on the floor and told him to go play with his toys.

Angry, the boy then went into the kitchen and suddenly screamed, letting Amra know he wants attention. She was pouring hot soup into a smaller pot at that time, got startled and spilled a lot of soup on the stove, which made her very angry. She raised her voice at the son, telling him to calm down because everything was hot, and someone could get hurt.

By this time, the boy was very angry. He went into his brother's bedroom and started crying loudly, intent on waking his brother up. It didn't take longer than a few seconds for him to do just that—his baby brother started crying as well. The noise alerted the father again, and he got up to lightly spank the older son while the mother, leaving the spilled soup and other mess in the kitchen, ran into the room, took the baby in her arms and started putting him back to sleep.

For a few seconds, maybe a whole minute, there was loud chaos in their apartment. However, the boy realised he overdid it, calmed down and went to play with his toys. The baby fell asleep soon again so the mother could go back to making lunch and the father tried once more to get some rest. And finally, there was peace. Or so they thought.

Not even 30 minutes later, someone knocked on their door. Amra hardly had time to open the door when two social workers roughly pushed their way into the apartment, looking for Amra and Stefan's older son. They told the shocked mother and father that they received an anonymous phone call from a neighbour about a boy screaming in the apartment. They were told there was a loud noise and based on that, a presumption was made that someone was abusing him.

Unsure whether this was some kind of a joke or not, the parents nicely told the social workers that it wasn't true, that the boy was crying a little bit and woke up his baby brother, nothing more. But the social workers would hear none of it. Their job, they told them, was to protect the child; that is, to take the child away from the parents momentarily and take him away for psychological and physical evaluation, to confirm whether the child was being subjected to any type of abuse or not.

As soon as the boy heard that, he started screaming again, clinging to his mother's apron, begging his parents not to let him go, promising he would be a good boy, that he'd never misbehave again. That was the only, genuine event that caused trauma to that little boy. That. Not his father spanking him or his mother yelling, but these two social workers, scary strangers showing up at the door and wanting to take him away. That scarred him for life.

Frightened parents wouldn't let them take their boy away, but the social workers wouldn't budge. By the law of the new country, they were legally not only allowed but expected to take the child away momentarily and put him into a foster home or with foster parents. Legally, all they needed, to act, was an anonymous report of child abuse, just a simple phone call. And that's exactly what they got, from an anonymous neighbour.

But both Amra and Stefan knew exactly who this neighbour was, the 'well' wishing spinster neighbour, the one who hated children and lived with a zillion cats. She always looked at children with disgust and rolled her eyes when any child was in proximity. Many parents in the building often waited for another elevator when they saw her go in, just to not be in the same elevator with her.

Anyhow, when Amra and Stefan realised this was no joke and that the social workers really did have the legal right to take their child away based solely on a telephone report of a malicious neighbour, Amra started sobbing while Stefan quickly grabbed his jacket and shoes and went along with the boy and the social workers to the Centre for Children and Family Services.

The next few hours were hell for that small family. The boy cried and sobbed like never before and never after, only wanting to go back home to play with his toys. *He'll be good, he promises. He'll be good, really. He'll never cry or be bad, he just wants to come back home.*

But first, the 'experts' at social care services had to examine him. Despite his father's objections, the boy had been examined by a doctor working for Social Services, to determine whether the boy had any bruises, scars, fresh scratches or whether he had been sexually molested. Then they took blood tests and urine to check if the child was being given any alcohol or drugs at home. All this time, the boy was screaming and crying uncontrollably, sobbing helplessly, and calling for his mom and dad.

They heard him. Amra, in her mother's heart, heard it while restlessly waiting at home with the baby. Stefan heard it, helplessly sitting in the waiting room, just across the examining room. He listened to his boy calling him, but all he could do is watch the closed door with tears running down his face—he could do nothing else. He wasn't allowed in there.

The social workers took the boy to the examining room alone and the father was told to wait in the waiting room, to prevent any child statements from being influenced by the father's presence. Father yelled for a while at the social workers, trying to explain to them what a shock this was for his boy, but the more he yelled and tried to explain, the more he realised that he was being labelled as emotionally or mentally unstable. Not as a father helplessly watching his son being traumatised while he could do nothing to protect him.

So, Stefan calmed down. Because if they thought that he was unstable, they would take his boy away. Just like that. So, the poor father had no choice, but to simply sit on that plastic chair in the waiting room, with his hands on top of his head, looking at the floor with tears falling down drop by drop. He could do nothing to help his son. Nothing.

She, on the other hand, was going through her own hell, wondering what was going on, constantly worrying about her older boy, how did all that happen, how could have all that happened… She couldn't understand any of it, it seemed like a nightmare in daylight, like the world was turned upside down in a blink of an eye. She was dumbfounded by it all. Had it all really happened?

Of course, all the tests done on the boy were fine and the social workers talked with the father, explaining to him the children's rights and his parental responsibilities. After all this torture, they finally let him go home with his son.

'The anonymous neighbour seemed to have made a mistake,'—that was the social workers' explanation, the excuse for the life-long trauma they caused this little boy.

When Stefan went home with his boy, it was already night. The baby was asleep at home. Although he was exhausted, neither he nor the boy could fall asleep. The boy was shaking, sobbing quietly and repeating to his parents that he'd be good, not to let anyone take him away, that he'd be good…they passed their hands gently over his face and his hair, teary-eyed themselves, assuring him they'll never let anyone take him away, that they love him, that he's their sun, their love, their world, their all.

The boy hugged his blue, ragged teddy bear and after almost 2 hours of crying, finally fell asleep. His father was supposed to work that night again but had to call in and let them know he wouldn't be able to come for his shift. He'd lose much-needed money, but they all went through a huge shock that day.

Amra and Stefan couldn't close their eyes all night. They still couldn't believe what had happened. They thought about the lady who made the anonymous report...the old neighbour who lived right across the hallway, the neighbour who always looked at their boys with disgust, the lady who said herself she prefers cats to children as cats don't talk back. She often complained that their boys were too loud, but they weren't loud, they were kids.

Kids don't speak calmly and slowly, kids speak playfully. That same neighbour lived with several cats, despite the rental agreement prohibiting pets. Ironically, Amra and Stefan knew keeping her cats was not permitted and that she'd be kicked out of the building if someone reported her, but they never did. They could have, though. They could have, easily. But they didn't. They knew that those cats meant everything to her, so they didn't want to cause her any problems or heartache. It never even occurred to them; it never even crossed their minds that *she* could do something so abominable to them, to their little boy.

They were 2 years short of being able to obtain the Canadian citizenship, but this situation made them realise that those documents were not the haven they expected or desired for themselves or their children. Suddenly, they were disgusted by it. Did they really want to become citizens of this kind of country, where a social worker was able to take a child away from the parents solely based on an anonymous report? No.

They realised they didn't want that citizenship, that the laws of the country were contradictory with the claim of being family-friendly, open and well-intended. They had to protect their children. The future in this country was not what they wished for their children. All that Canada gave them, it seems, was a false promise. Or, perhaps, definitions and expectations were drastically different in the two worlds known to them—the one they came from and the Canadian one.

So, they rushed to collect money for one-way airplane tickets. Some they borrowed from friends, some they had themselves and, already that week, they returned to Greece. They enrolled the boy in kindergarten where he picked up the language really fast. Stefan continued to make decent money painting portraits in the streets and Amra went for quiet long walks with their younger son. They realised that sometimes, taking several steps back is when you gain the biggest advantage. And as far as a better future goes, they realised they needed to enjoy every today because tomorrow is the future for today.

This statement, as cliché as it sounds, was the guiding light of some other people we met. For them, Canada really was the promised land, because it distanced them from their past physically, if not psychologically. You can leave the ghost land but leaving the ghosts behind is a lifelong aim. However, they kept going for their children, doing everything they could, putting themselves last to provide the best they could for their children, to make sure their children would always be protected, safe, and loved.

Two women that I vividly remember to this day are Ms R and Ms Em. Ms R had a baby girl when we first met her. She always kept to herself, politely greeting, but quietly. That baby girl had so much love poured into her by that woman! I cannot remember a single moment ever seeing Ms R alone, without her daughter.

As with all Balkan people, everyone was curious about everyone—after all, we were all in the same situation, foreigners in Canada. We already felt a sort of allegiance, so asking random and personal questions was normal. With that in mind, everyone inquired about Ms R's husband, partner, baby's father, but she never spoke of him. She'd just quietly say 'He died' and walk on. It was quite a strange thing to do.

We belong to a mentality where everyone must know what everyone eats for breakfast, and whom everyone sleeps with—it's a very nosy mentality that's not intentionally nosy but simply made that way. But Ms R never talked about it. Once, I saw her sitting down in a park, pensively looking at the stroller, wiping a tear that involuntarily fell from her eye.

God's Gift

Ms R. never forgot the event. She never forgot his ferocious eyes, his vicious laughter, feeding off her pleading, sobbing, screaming. She was completely helpless. She had no one to help. Her entire family was killed moments before.

She could never forget his one hand holding her down, while his other hand unbuttoned his pants. The pain, the smell of blood and freshly burned homes, the feeling of being suffocated by helplessness, all these were merged into a horrible memory, now labelled as 'the event'. She tried so hard to force it into oblivion and every time something reminded her of it, she used every ounce of her effort to push it to the back of her mind. Still, when she occasionally touched the bedside table in her sleep, she'd shudder and wake up in a panic.

All these years later, she still couldn't fathom that it happened. Or why it happened. She just couldn't understand it. Her brother and father were killed, her mother as well, she was raped, their home destroyed, dreams and plans crushed, hearts ripped out…simply because they belonged to a 'wrong' religion. Just like many other compatriots, they were victims of ethnical cleansing… 'simply because'…an unreasonable excuse for an unjustifiable act of cruelty.

She remembered his panting, intermittent laughter and his words, that he'd make her an Ethnic child. It was all so tragic…

She tried to think of a different scenario, some normal circumstances in which she could have met this man. For instance, a grocery store. In normal circumstances, she could've met this man there. They could've exchanged shy smiles. He could've asked her out for a coffee. She could've accepted. They could've fallen in love. He could've proposed to her in the most romantic way. They could've gotten married. They could've made love and could have had a beautiful love child.

It wouldn't have mattered if that love child's father was Serbian, Bosnian, or Croatian. If he were Roman Catholic, Jewish, Muslim, or Orthodox. Their love is all that would've mattered. It could've been done that way. It could have.

Instead, this man raped her, killed her family and burned her home down in order to make her an Ethnic child. All this, simply because she was not of the same religion as he was, the same nationality. They spoke the same language, walked the same grounds, shared the same homeland. Why did it have to be done this way? Why was it necessary to inflict all that misery and pain, all those infinite emotional and physical scars? To prove some point?

She was raised to respect all people, regardless of their colour, origin or religion. Why did he expect to humiliate her by making her an Ethnic child? It was a ridiculous thought. He thought that the fact she might have an Ethnic child is what she should be humiliated about. Not the brutal rape, not the atrocities he did, but the fact she might have an Ethnic child.

She survived the ordeal, the event. She escaped to the homeland's capital, where she realised that she was pregnant. She thought about all the options, but realistically, she had no doubts as to what she would do. She was young, in her early 20s and had a whole life in front of her. Perhaps it was a life full of scars, carved deep into her body and soul, but a life, nonetheless. Ironically, she was fortunate, compared to so many other people who were never given the option to choose between life and death. There were so many people who lost a leg, who lost their right arm, who lost an eye, who lost the ability to have children, lost the ability to love but didn't feel hate nonetheless... They all continued living. Vegetating, perhaps, but participating in life, nonetheless.

How could she not? Compared to such brave people who chose life with all its obstacles, she would be incredibly rude, to say the least, to cowardly choose death, for her or for the child she was carrying. Even now when she did in fact carry an Ethnic child. It was her child too, nonetheless.

The logical option for most people would be for her to abort. She was young, raped in war by an enemy soldier. It was logical to remove not only the inside of her uterus but the uterus itself, to remove every physical remnant and reminder of that act, of that very event. It was logical that she ends up in a psychiatric institution, to do a lifetime of counselling, sobbing over her destiny, sobbing over becoming an orphan at the same time most of her peers globally were leading a life full of joy, careless fun...very different from her own.

It was logical for her to eventually marry someone of her own religion, and harbour hate, mildly said, towards any Ethnic members in her homeland, in neighbouring countries, neighbouring continents, all over the world. Simply put, it was logical and expected of her to hate everyone, based on the pain caused to her by one of them. To hate everyone else for not preventing it. To hate herself too. It was logical for most people, but not for her.

She was, you could say, much stronger psychologically than one would expect a girl of her age to be, especially in those circumstances. She was much braver than one would admit. Or just plain insane, as many had then said of her. 'Traumatised...she couldn't know what she was doing.' But she did. She knew that if she aborted that child, that innocent life in her womb, she would only punish that poor, innocent soul. She would not punish him, the rapist.

Only he could be his own greatest punishment. He had to wake up every morning and look at his face in the mirror and face a new day of haunting memories of the atrocities he did. Sooner, or later. That was the greatest punishment of all, she thought. And aborting that child would not erase the event. She herself would not be free of that memory. Nothing magical would happen for her, her life would turn into no butterflies, unicorns, or seventh heaven. The event could never be undone.

Would killing him, the rapist, do anything? No. It would help him by ending his torment. Make no mistake, his torment would show up, even if he felt no regret immediately.

Would torturing and massacring him help? No. On the contrary, it could turn him into a victim. Would removing her uterus and removing the baby help her? No. The emotional scar would never heal anyway, so why would she additionally punish herself by adding another scar to her already suffering soul?

The best way she could punish him was to continue living as normally as she possibly could. So, she did. That is when that baby inside of her womb became her baby and her baby alone. She moved to Canada as an immigrant and started a new life. She gave birth to a beautiful, healthy baby girl and named her Alma, meaning 'soul'. No part of a human being could be alive and well if their soul was not. *Mens sana in corpore sano*...she recalled a physical education class from her high school days. She was determined to have a healthy soul, and that soul would be her daughter.

When people asked her who the father was, she only replied that he died in the war. Most people were mannered enough not to continue prying, and when only a couple of times someone still decided to comment something about that, she'd say she never talked about it. That would end all questions.

At first, she lived off of social assistance, like all other immigrants, until her daughter grew bigger. Eventually, she enrolled her in kindergarten and started working. Bit by bit, they were merging with the local culture, shedding old skin and gaining a new, healthier looking one.

Her daughter was growing into a beautiful, compassionate, loving and smart little girl. How could she not? She infused her with all the love she had, loved her with every ounce of her being, and channelled all her positive energy, hope and joy into that little girl. She was raising her into a wonderful human being. She was all she had.

Occasionally, she remembered 'the event'. Occasionally, she would instinctively want to scream if someone patted her on the shoulder. Occasionally, her scar would give her a sharp, sudden pain. Like forgetting you have a healed cut on your foot until you accidentally step on something right in that spot and the pain gets reactivated. That's how it was for her.

She didn't socialise much at first. She never socialised with people from her homeland or anyone who spoke her mother tongue. That was one way to keep her memories of the event dormant. And to keep people from prying. Instead, she socialised with other mothers, especially single moms in Canada, and learned to live a more carefree life, at least on the outside. With time, she learned to control her emotions and kept channelling them into all the positive she could think of—her daughter, Alma.

She never went back to her homeland. Perhaps it was cowardly of her not to, wrong. It seemed like she forgot about her distant family, forgot about the innocent lives taken away. But she could not go back not because she forgot about them, but because she *didn't* forget about them. And because she didn't forget about the event. That was the problem. She tried to and kept trying. Every day, every hour, every minute. But she didn't forget. She simply couldn't.

For that reason, she could not go back. She thought of her family's remains every day, in the dark of the night, in the whiteness of her dreams, in the blackness of her nightmares, she thought of them all the time. But she knew they were well, resting in heaven and looking down on her. She knew they didn't judge her; they raised her to be as she was, strong and loving despite all life's troubles. And she was living exactly that way.

Perhaps her story was unusual, perhaps her actions were difficult to fathom. But she knew she was doing everything right every time she looked into her daughter's loving and smiling eyes. Ironically, that highly traumatising event gave her a true blessing—a reason to live, a will to fight the demons of the past, and the strength to overcome anything.

Likewise, Ms M was the very epitome of this strength. My family, and some others, knew her from back home. They knew her husband too, all too well. He was a notorious drunk, one of those who hates himself in the morning and hates the rest of the world in the evening. Did he have his own story? Probably, everyone has one. But this story is about his wife, Ms M. She was a journalist who used to model when she was young.

He was a well-known photographer, and that's how they met. Initially, he'd 'just' slap her. Soon, the slapping turned into heavy hits that flew her to the ground. A few pulled-out hairs turned into several broken teeth. Then, it was her jaw, her arm, her leg. When the war started, the hits she received intensified as much as the sniper hits. One of those sniper hits got her husband, and suddenly—she was free. In the middle of a besieged city, with no food, electricity or water, with grenades exploding daily, she felt liberated. She felt free. The first opportunity she had, she left the homeland with their baby son and arrived to Canada.

The Mask

It was morning. Still half-asleep, Ms M was standing in front of the mirror and asking herself: 'Who will I be today?' She was looking at her jaded face, dark circles under her eyes, wrinkles, adult acne on her chin, pocks on the forehead, red eyes, thinning lips, scar on her cheek. While reaching for the cosmetic pouch, she concluded, once again, it was better to be anyone but herself.

She took a yellow concealer out of the cosmetic pouch and slowly spat the dark under-eye circles. It was as if with every swipe of her hand she wished to defeat them; not only conceal but completely erase them from her face. It wasn't that she was bothered by the under-eye circles per se or their purplish colour.

On the contrary, the purple colour always beautifully emphasised her chestnut-coloured eyes. The problem lay in what those dark circles represented and revealed about her life, about her. They were a reminder, evidence, and result of a myriad of sleepless nights; black nights that kept her awake, not because of some passionate love affair she could only read about in romance novels, but because of the burden of real life, daily problems.

Suddenly, her hand slowed down and rested on the bathroom counter, still holding the concealer while the woman recalled one of those many nights when she was lying down in a freezing room on a cold and hard mattress. She was so petrified that she didn't even feel the cold prowling under her bones.

She remembered looking at the cracked ceiling that leaked; she remembered the breathing noise of her infant son, lying in a crib beside her. She remembered his little tuft, peeking from under a few, thin blankets she covered her precious baby with. She remembered the night in which she feared the day because that new day wasn't bringing anything new, anything better.

Her rebellious hand suddenly went up towards the dark circles, firmly grasping the concealer, squeezing it like the best friend who could change everything, erase everything, force everything into oblivion.

She returned the somewhat overused yellow concealer to the pouch and took out a green concealer with which she made a few gentle swipes over the red scar on her cheek. The swipes were so slow, so soft, as if their gentleness could take away the pain that resulted in the making of the scar. But the green concealer couldn't take away the memory…memory of another black night infused with the aroma of alcohol, sweat and steel blood, salty tears and a heavy hand of one, once very dear man. At least, she could conceal the outer redness, the outer stamp. She put the concealer down on the counter.

For a moment, she paused, looked at herself in the mirror and took a deep breath. She pensively regarded her face, acne on her chin. She raised her fingers towards them, to destroy them, squeeze them, to even out the skin. Suddenly, she stopped. She raised her eyes towards the pocks on her forehead. She smiled. She looked at the chin acne again, then back at the pocked forehead, a sort of 'before' and 'after' versions. She thought of the day she squeezed out her first zit. She was about 12 years old.

On one hand, that zit was a messenger of the grown-up times to come—the period, bigger breasts, make-up and high heels. On the other hand, that zit was a nasty giant on her face, a face that sat right behind a blue-eyed Evan. With that zit, she couldn't even look at Evan! And so, one day, she squeezed that giant out. Other zits were squeezed because of Miran, Ivan, Danilo…and each one of those crushes was and remained just one big nothing. A hole, just like pocks on her forehead.

She returned the green concealer to the cosmetic pouch, taking out a powder foundation. She put a powder brush in her other hand and dived it into the powder foundation. With flaky movements, she applied powder to her face, like a cloud of skin-coloured cotton smoke. She successfully got rid of sporadic redness on her face, but no matter how hard she tried to drown the wrinkles with her powder, she couldn't. As if they were a bottomless river, streaming through her face.

No amount of powder could drain their spring. Today…today, they defeated her… Or did they? Was she to surrender that easily? Was she to let the passers-by see so openly and so clearly, all her wounds of life written right on her face? Forehead wrinkles created by too many worries, wrinkles around lips created as a result of numerous tirades, crow's feet formed by too many tears…should she let everyone see her life story, pain and heartache? No! She put the powder brush back into the cosmetic pouch and took out a skin-coloured corrector pencil. She took a cotton swab, gently scrubbed the surface of the corrector pencil and then used it to fill in the riverbanks on her face. She did this once, then again, then again and then again.

She threw the cotton swab in the garbage, put the corrector pencil back into the cosmetic pouch, took out the powder and the brush again and once more, she gently enwrapped her face with the powder smoke. She looked at her face and took a deep, triumphant breath.

She returned the powder and brush to the pouch, taking out her favourite, indigo eye shadow. How wonderful it used to look on her eyes! It's not that it didn't look nice now; her eyes were still the colour of chestnut. But the garden her irises lived in had changed colour. Once upon a time, her chestnut eyes were like brown leaves in a cotton bouquet, whereas today, they looked more like ash in a grimed fireplace.

She wasn't surprised by her regard, however; she's been waking up with those tired eyes for years now. As if her eyes, after all they've seen, simply decided to turn red, what of anger, what of frustration, sadness, and helplessness. She put the eye shadow down on the counter, took a bottle of eye drops and put a few drops in each eye. She put the bottle back on the shelf, took another cotton swab and gently absorbed the runaway drops. A few blinks at the mirror and her eyes once again became the shiny chestnuts in a cotton garden. Finally, she made a few moves with her eye shadow and put on mascara.

She then took a lip plumper and applied it, feeling tingling on her lips. She remembered the days when her lips felt those tingles after a juicy, sweet kiss; that passionate, sudden, innocently sinful kiss. Those used to be the tingles of sweet happiness. Today, they are the tingles of necessary pain. However, her lips did look like she had just been kissed, only by a bee.

She used a small sponge to apply bronzer to her cheeks, forehead, nose, and chin. She put the makeup back into the pouch and closed it. She put it away gently, on the shelf under the mirror, very carefully, as if that pouch was the most prized of all her possessions. Like it was her very best friend. That one friend you can always count on.

Once more, feeling simultaneous fear and hope, she raised her head towards the mirror, looking at the face of the woman looking back at her. Intently, she spent a moment looking at every corner, every bit of her reflection, from the eyebrow to the overall impression. The face of the woman in the mirror has become rested, cheerful, younger, and happier. It became the way it should naturally be, the way it decided to feel today.

It is true, then, that the natural make-up application consumed the most time. She knew that she spent too much time, too much of her life, to acquire that natural feeling, to create that natural look, the look a woman of her age should naturally have, the look and the feeling she too would naturally have had not *all* the life's troubles knocked on her door…

'Mom, are you done yet? I need the bathroom too! What are you doing in there? I've got the bar exam today, have you forgotten? I've got to get ready!' she heard her son from the other side of the bathroom door.

'No, I didn't forget, how could I? I'll be right out!' She replied with a smile. She also smiled to the woman in the mirror, as if telling her: 'Today, we conquered everything that is yesterday. Let's step into tomorrow!'

She opened the bathroom door and bravely walked out, with a natural mask on her face.

For others, it was not so easy to put a mask on and pretend it is all well. What of age, what of frustration…it was not easy to pretend. The Old Man, for instance, spent most of his life in Canada, fell in love with his wife and raised his children there, only to have his children assimilate too much, to the point of moving away so far that they hardly saw him once a year, if that.

Like most Canadian children, the Old Man's children also moved out when they were 18, against his and his wife's will. They started working and eventually, moved with their own families across the country. The Old Man was left alone, widowed and practically childless, having worked his whole life to provide for his family, to keep them close, to keep them happy and satisfied. Or so he thought…and then, the lowest point of his life befell him.

The Final Humiliation

Humiliation. What else can be said but utter humiliation, like a poisonous cherry on top of something that should've been a delicious ice cream sundae. Albeit that was not it, from the very beginning. From the very first day of his arrival, the Old Man has been systematically humiliated. Discretely, of course, because after all, this was the country that strictly prohibited discrimination in theory, but fully allowed it in practice. The country that showed full respect to immigrants in theory but showed full humiliation in practice. But it's the new glass ceiling…one cannot go against it.

The only way for you to understand that it does exist is to touch it. The Old Man has already been used to those petty, daily, chronic humiliations. But this…this was the peak, the ultimate humiliation he didn't expect to be subjected to at the age of 83, almost nearing an exit from life.

He came to Canada over 50 years ago, out of necessity. He got married here, had children. Children were so beautifully assimilated, that they were ashamed of their father's background. Not openly, but on any inquiries about their father's background, they always emphasised they were born and raised in Canada, avoiding the reply, the fact, that their father was not. They were ashamed to the point that they changed their last name to make it sound more English.

Avoiding the fact that their father was born and raised in what then was the country called Czechoslovakia. The problem didn't lie in Czechoslovakia per se. The same shame would appear if it were any other country in the world, any other but Canada itself. If you were a 'native' in Canada, the 10th generation of Canadians, everything was fine. But if you weren't, then you only were and could be an immigrant, regardless of the time spent in the country, be it 6 months or 60 years.

Once an immigrant in the eyes of Canada, always an immigrant in the eyes of Canada. An immigrant until you die and then your descendants, born in Canada, continued to be brainwashed day by day until they become completely and irrevocably assimilated into the new so-called Canadian 'culture'. And forget their backgrounds.

That's how it was for the Old Man. So many times, he regretted leaving his homeland, but there was no going back. He was already old, had an ill prostate and was counting down the hours of his life on Earth. Hours, not years or days. Just hours. He had to walk with the help of a cane.

Thinking of his homeland, he couldn't help but get teary-eyed. He had a good life there, not in financial terms, but people recognised and valued him as a human being, worthy of respect. His life was valued by more than a social security number. He was a university professor with a PhD. degree, and although even in Canada he obtained a university professor position, it included inevitable daily doses of petty humiliations.

Also, his wife was laid to her final resting place in Canada; his children were here, although there were both emotionally and physically distant. But they were here. It was easier for him to walk the same grounds as his children, even if they were so many miles between them.

Today, though, the humiliation he was subjected to was so appalling, so horrendous, that it made him sob for who knows what time, asking God why he hadn't taken him already and saved him from such tyranny. Because at his age, humiliation was not humiliation anymore, but pure tyranny.

Going for a stroll in his neighbourhood, his ailing bladder warned him to hurry back home. He wasn't as before; he wasn't capable of self-control. However, with all those daily humiliations, wearing adult diapers was the last thing the Old Man wanted or intended to do. His dignity had already been taken away from him, should he succumb to wearing diapers too? No. He would not be put in diapers because this little bit of self-respect was all he had left.

The Old Man had to hurry home, as fast as he possibly could. He firmly grasped his cane, his best and most faithful friend, and hurried home, limping. He couldn't get to the marked street crossing, it was too far, and even if he did cross the street at the designated place, he'd still have to walk back the entire block. He was in a great hurry; his bladder was counting down seconds.

The Old Man stopped walking, looked to the right and the left of the street, through the thick lenses of his prescription glasses, and as no cars were approaching from either side, the Old Man decided to cross the street at an unmarked crossing. He was in a hurry, there were no cars…who'd mind? But someone did.

Namely, on the other side of the street, from a small distance, he was preyed on by two testosterone-pumped policewomen. They were the authority; in their uniforms, they were 'somebody'. And they had a strong need to prove the point, to enforce their authority on someone. But whom? On an immigrant… on an 83-year-old immigrant.

On seeing him jaywalk, they approached him with their cowboy walk and asked him in their rough, deep voices, whether he was aware he had just broken the law by jaywalking. He replied in fluent English, but with a thick accent, that he had an ailing bladder and that he needed to hurry home. But they wouldn't let him go. Their rough voices brusquely told him not to raise his voice at them. But he wasn't raising his voice at them.

He spoke with a thick, Eastern European accent, with a mixed feeling of panic, helplessness and despair, he was trying to explain to them that he had to rush, that he had to get to a toilet. They mistook his verbal struggle for disobedience. They were the authority, after all. And they had to take it out on an 83-year-old grandpa.

Had his name been John Smith, had he been able in fluent non-accented English to explain why he had to hurry, there wouldn't have been any problems. But even when he only breathed pure air, the Old Man, like all other immigrants, was looked at as a potential problem. Low-class citizen.

Taking his cane away from him, the policewomen put his hands behind his back, handcuffed him and pushed him against the side door of their police car. What authority! A few drops of blood shyly appeared from his soft, old chin. Slowly, his bladder couldn't hold tears either. The Old Man realised that finally, after more than 50 years, Canada succeeded in taking away from him the last crumb of dignity he had left.

Everything was over. He was defeated. He was taken in the back of the car, like the worst criminal; handcuffed, with his prescription eyeglasses bent, his chin bloodied and worst of all, wet pants—trampled dignity. He used to be a university professor with a PhD, a man who never crushed an ant intentionally. But who did that matter to now, what was it all worth now? Nothing. One big nothing. Because he wasn't John Smith.

Ironically, not being John Smith in Canada, was just as bad as being a Gypsy in my homeland. But the couple who lived on the 2nd floor of our rental building never believed in class, race or any other differences. From day one, they were honest and open, with themselves and the world around them. Their love story endured their past and their present but didn't reach their future. For them, war provided a glimpse of hope that the new beginning they were forced to make would be a good one. But their happily ever after wasn't it. Life plays strange games sometimes.

Love Story

'If you walk out this door, you can forget you ever had parents!' were their last words. The very last words he heard from them, the very last time he saw them. Now lying on a hospital bed on a different continent, with just days left to live, Zlatan recalled those words. He thought of how big of a punishment it would be for them to know that he died, those words being the last ones they ever told him. He wondered whether they deserved to live with that guilt. He did openly disobey them; he did choose love over the common sense of his birth society.

His love was a hairstylist named Anita, a Gypsy, who worked in a tiny, cheap hair salon in a not-so-glitzy part of Sarajevo. He was a computer engineer with a master's degree, at a time when most didn't even know what a computer was. He grew up in the very city centre in a family of esteemed lawyers. As a couple, two of them together were an inoperable disease, an unmatchable mix, water and fire, cotton and cactus, stallion and lizard, they did not go together—everyone said so.

In a wannabe aristocratic society with many elements of pompousness, having a man of his status even talk to a woman of her status was considered a greater woe than a deadly disease.

Ironically…now he truly had an inoperable disease, cancer cells throughout his body, eating him up alive. He wondered if now he'd receive some pardon, some release of his 'sin'.

He never regretted his decision, despite all the tough times he and she had gone through, despite the many downs and problems that awaited them every step of the way. The few ups, the few little battles won, the many laughs and immense love they felt, always made it worth every tear they shed, every scar they won together.

No, she was not from an educated family, nor did she go to university. She was who she was, with no pretence made. Ever. She was a Gypsy, she did only have a hair styling certificate, she was fairly poor, and she did grow up in a half-torn house with another 12 members of her family. She never made any pretence about it. Being a Gypsy, though, contrary to the popular belief, didn't make her a thief, a prostitute, a criminal, or a contagious disease.

She worked hard to contribute to her family's budget, like everyone else; to put food on the table, pay for utilities. She didn't beg on the streets. She worked hard. Yet she never let herself think she needed or deserved Manolos or a mansion. She never had any unrealistic expectations or desires. She always returned anything she found that didn't belong to her, she helped older people cross the street, at least those that didn't shun her immediately, she did pick up and hand back anything that another person dropped, and she called for help if she'd see someone in trouble.

But despite it all, people always just saw her as a dirty, disease-laden, criminal activity oriented—Gypsy. No matter what she'd do, she'd always remain just that. Legally, there was no discrimination, racism and similar allowed, but in practice, there was a glass ceiling that wasn't even made of clear but tinted glass. Everyone could see it.

When he fell in love with her, he fell in love with her just for that. For being who she was. For being beautiful, open, honest, diligent, true to her words and her heart. Too many women in his milieu were pretenders, only fishing after a good match. But Anita put love first, trust first. They met by accident, in a little coffee shop outside the city centre. She was sitting there with a co-worker; Zlatan was there by himself. He noticed her immediately.

In a pool of white faces and fake blondes with caked makeup, her natural beauty stood out. She had tanned skin, shoulder-length dark hair, large brown eyes and a huge, sincere smile. She was serious but easy going. She was being herself. And right then and there, he fell in love with her. He waited until her friend went to the bathroom, moved to her table and started up a conversation. She was very reluctant to start up a relationship with him, fully aware of the societal constrictions.

Ultimately believing that love should not be meddled with, she surrendered and let her heart lead her. They knew that the love they had was one of a kind and that letting it go through their fingers would be the real sin. Their biggest troubles began when they both realised they wanted to spend the rest of their lives together.

Her parents thought she would just get hurt, that she had her head in the clouds, that she was his temporary toy. His parents saw her as a thief who was slyly trying to get into their lives, perhaps even to kill them to inherit their material possessions. The poles they grew up on were too far apart. He knew that if they wanted to be together, they would have to do it on their own.

So, they did. They moved in together, rented out a small apartment in a cheap part of town and got married in the city hall. All by themselves. She didn't have a big wedding, she didn't even have any wedding cake or a wedding dress, there was no wedding banquet, no guests, no congratulations or good wishes, no wedding gifts, no rice thrown at them for good luck.

Not even a flower bouquet, just one little daisy flower he picked up for her. Nonetheless, it was the most beautiful wedding in the world because it was the sincerest one—their love was at the centre of attention, with no side distractions. She continued working in the same salon; he continued working for the same institute, occasionally under fire of mal-intended comments regarding his new wife. But he bit his tongue and continued working because he needed the job, his family having completely disowned him. He and his new wife had no one but themselves.

They and they alone were responsible for putting their own food on the table, finding a roof over their head. He was cut from all the inheritance, and she had nothing to inherit, so to buy any kind of home of their own they would have had to work really, really hard. Especially, if they planned on having children—which they did.

After a few years have passed, they were able to get a mortgage and bought a tiny apartment on the outskirts of

Sarajevo. She had given birth to their first child, a beautiful baby girl whom they saw as the crown of their love.

They spent all their free time together; there were no moments spent apart except for when they worked. They really were the best friends, the loyal couple, devoted spouses, loving parents; they genuinely embodied all those values that many consider clichés. Their neighbours often saw them walking around the building with their daughter, hugging, laughing, holding hands, playing with her. Although openly most people scorned and judged their relationship, they peeked behind the curtains, wistfully admiring that genuine love.

Because most, you see, didn't have the courage to disregard, to break free from societal constraints. Most did what they were told they ought to do, what was acceptable for them to do. Sooner or later, most regretted it. But Anita and Zlatan, they did only what their hearts told them to do. And they never, ever looked back.

Occasionally, they would see his parents on the streets of the city. And every time, his parents would cross to the other side of the street or enter a store, just to avoid meeting them. They didn't care about the granddaughter they had, they didn't care about their son or any aspect of his life. Instead of being proud parents for raising a good human being, they were ashamed of him. It would have been more acceptable had he turned out to be a man with a 'nose' for a good match, for not only respecting the values he was born into but looking for ways to expand them. Values meaning material matters…status…real estate…wealth.

Zlatan expected them to act that way. Although, he was sad…somewhere deep inside. Mostly though, he felt sorry for them because they were the ones stuck under that self-imposed glass ceiling instead of truly living the only life they'll ever have. He was happy, and that was all that mattered.

Unfortunately, that feeling of happiness was short-lived as one day, Sarajevo found itself under siege. War started very soon afterwards, and their part of town, being on the outskirts of Sarajevo, was the least protected and the first one to fall into enemy hands. In a matter of days, they lost their little apartment, their hard-earned little piece of heaven; the little peace, happiness and security they created for themselves with blood and sweat. It was all gone. All of it. All the hard work they endured for years, just to be able to buy that tiny apartment.

It was all gone. They never even saw it happen though because as soon as the first siren sounded, they were moved into the underground shelter where they spent several months while the city was being viciously attacked. He would occasionally sneak out with a few other people from the shelter, to get food aid during the few moments of the ceasefire, most of which was constantly broken. Often, fewer people would come back to the shelter than had left.

Zlatan was lucky to return every time. Eventually, an underground tunnel was dug up through which people were able to obtain food, or go to a different part of town, different shelter. It was risky but much safer than getting out of the shelter, as the enemy had already taken over that part of town. Whoever went out of the shelter would be killed. Actually, killed is a humane way to put it, as being killed would mean a simple bullet or a deadly stab, but these people didn't 'simply' kill.

Realising that the war would not end soon and that the defending forces had no means to defend themselves with, Anita and Zlatan chose to take a lesser risk and leave for the other area of town through the secret tunnel. They then decided to try to leave their city with one of the UNPROFOR convoys. They were blessed with a little fortune, and they did arrive to safety with their daughter.

They had very little money with them but received refugee status and assistance immediately. They had no place to live and were happy to find for rent a little room outside the town, which they were able to afford from the refugee assistance.

It was impossible to live like this. They couldn't obtain jobs. She was still a Gypsy, from war-ravaged Bosnia, and those two combined made her almost an equivalent of a woman with leprosy. Everyone avoided her. He was from war-ravaged Bosnia, married to a Gypsy, but a computer engineer, so his chances to obtain any employment were slightly better, although in those conditions—minimal. She started working as a cleaning lady as no one cared what a cleaner looked like.

They were just people who cleaned up bathrooms after others have used them; they cleaned garbage cans after others have filled them with their junk. Now that—that a Gypsy could do. But she was a modest, hardworking woman: she believed there was no shame in doing any honest job. She was not selling her body for money or stealing; she was cleaning. Her husband though still had no job. Someone had to take care of their daughter anyhow, so he stayed at home.

Somehow, despite all the precautions, she realised she was pregnant again. It was certainly not the time to have another child but having an abortion or putting the child up for adoption was never an option, not even a remote one. Not even in those circumstances. Still, they could not bring another child into these living and working conditions, into this situation. Soon, they applied for immigrant status to a few foreign countries hoping for a better, more perspective life. That's how they came to Canada, where they started smiling again, although slowly and cautiously.

Still, their smiles became perceptible again. Upon arrival, they received landed immigrant status, health insurance, social assistance and accommodation for the first 1-2 months until they find their own place. Within a few weeks, they rented their own apartment, bigger than any place they've ever had in their life as spouses—almost a 500 square feet one bedroom apartment.

The government even supplied them with furniture for the entire apartment, all the basics from the utensils to the bed and table and chairs. They couldn't believe it. It seemed like finally; they were getting a break from all their misfortunes. Compared to what they came from, for them—this *was* a dream come true, furniture and all.

She gave birth to their second daughter, another blessing. They hoped that perhaps her birth symbolised a beginning of a new life, a carefree, judgement-free life for them all.

She obtained employment as a part-time hair stylist, so she could be with children the rest of the time. He found full-time employment as a computer engineer and started earning decent money. They were able to get off social assistance. She ceased working completely to spend all her time with the children.

Occasionally, she would still do haircuts at home for a few neighbours. It was just on occasion and not well-paid, but she couldn't stave off the feeling that any bit of extra money would help. She just never wanted to go through the same uncertainty or helpless situation ever again.

In Canada, people didn't look at her as a Gypsy. For all they knew, she could've been a Filipino, a Latin-American, African American, or a Native. For all they cared, she could've been a Marsonian. It didn't matter. It didn't matter who Anita and Zlatan were or where they came from. They were simply numbers. All that mattered was how well they worked and how well they assimilated into the new Canadian culture and its way of life. And they both did that really well. Their children were citizens of the country in every meaning of that word. They were growing up unaware of the existence of racial intolerance, blissfully happy to be just who they were.

Another few years passed by and they all received full citizenship.

They socialised occasionally with very, very few compatriots. Occasionally, they'd get the word that their families back home were well, except for one of Anita's brothers, who died in the war. No one notified her. For her family, she was as good as dead. In their eyes, she betrayed them, and she knew them well enough to know that it would be futile to even try and make amends with them. Besides, that belonged to some other life she led before coming to Canada. Now, she was finally happy, and nothing could hurt them.

But these two lovely people had no idea that their troubles were far from over.

When her husband went for an annual medical check-up, as it was required for all employees of the company he worked for, doctors didn't like the blood test results. They sent him for more tests until a few days later they told him he had metastasised leukaemia and only days, a few weeks at the most to live. Out of the blue. He did increasingly feel weak and tired and was paler every day, but he thought it was just because he worked so much.

It never occurred to him that he could be ill. They've gone through so much, and they finally found peace here. This *was* the piece of heaven they earned. And everyone's well in heaven, right? No one is ill in heaven, no one dies in heaven, right?

What did they mean, he had leukaemia? Only days, a few weeks at the most, to live? That was ridiculous, preposterous. That just couldn't be. It just simply had to be a mistake. Maybe they switched his test results with someone else's…it had to be some mistake!

But it was no mistake.

As his condition worsened in days, just like the doctors said, he ended up in a hospital. He found himself on the very same bed he was still on right now, waiting for death to come and take him away from the little piece of happiness he worked so damn hard for. Why was he so cursed, so frowned upon by someone up there, whoever it is that dictates our destiny? Didn't he suffer enough already? Didn't she suffer enough? Didn't they deserve to enjoy some peace? They just wanted to live as a family. To modestly, quietly, enjoy their life as a family. Why would someone up there not allow that? It was not right. They were good people. Good.

He thought of his wife, who was constantly by his side, trying to hide the tears the best she could, although the swollen eyes made her feelings hard to conceal. She knew though, she had to keep herself together as the two children they had would have no one in the world except her. And she needed all the possible strength in the world to get through this and raise them into loving, intelligent women.

His children came to visit him on occasion, on his better days only, as he wanted them to remember him the way he was before—strong, defiant, loving, happy, funny, protective. Not the way he was now—defeated, drained out, a living dead.

A few days before he died, Anita came to the hospital with his phone book. She gave it to him and they exchanged a tearful look. He never said anything all those years, but she knew that deep inside, he loved his parents very much. Although he was hurt by their behaviour, it would not be right for him to go to the grave knowing how much they'd suffer on realising he'd died, their last words to him having been the worst possible ones. And his expulsion from their home, their hearts being his last memory of them.

She brought a prepaid international phone card with her and dialled the number for him because he was too weak to do it himself. She then put the phone to his ear. After a few rings, his father answered the phone.

He said 'Hello, dad', and started crying. His father remained silent but didn't hang up. He imagined that the father was likely holding onto a chair or wall, shocked to hear his son's voice.

'Hello dad… It's me. I know we ended on bad terms, but I am calling to say that I forgave you and that I want you to remember that. I do not hold it against you, and I love you all, nonetheless. I have the most wonderful wife and two beautiful children and do not regret choosing them and choosing love, but I…' His speech got interrupted by tears and laboured breathing, '…I am at a hospital, I have leukaemia…a few days left here…' that's when he heard his father sob uncontrollably on the other side of the phone line. 'I just want to tell you and mother and everyone that I forgive you, that's all. I didn't want to die knowing you'll have to live with that…and it is Anita who's responsible for this phone call…'

'…and I am just so sorry you never gave her or us a chance, you missed out on so much, but I forgive you. And I wish you met our girls, they are…everything…our sunshine. I forgive you all… Goodbye.'—He hung up, sobbing. He just didn't have any strength left.

On the other side of the world, his father fell into a baroque-style armchair, sobbing, with the handset still in his hand. His son forgave him…but he knew he could never forgive himself. Ever.

Two days after that, Zlatan died. He kissed his wife and saw his children for the very last time and then fell asleep forever. His wife never remarried, and to this day, she visits his grave every single day. Their daughters are all grown up, educated, and married with children. He would be so proud of them. She was happy that their girls grew up into successful young women by all standards. But what she was proud of the most and knew he would be proud of the most, was that they grew up into honest, fair, loving and caring young women. And no money could ever buy that.

Another thing that no money could ever buy is good memories. When life takes a sharp turn, we tend to retreat to good memories and find solace in them. I often did that, and so did my parents, their friends, my friends, everyone I know. We often talked about how good life was in our homeland, before the war and once the war ended as well. Compared to life in Canada, our war-stricken, injured homeland was still so much better for living, more inviting, welcoming, more honest.

Our homeland would welcome you with open arms and share the little it has with you, even if you were a complete stranger. It has always been that kind of a country, even after the war. The country with a soul and heart. But the people back home didn't realise that. We knew, because we know both sides of the story, we lived through them in every possible sense. However, explaining it to someone back home was useless…for them, the grass is always greener on the other side. Especially, if it's a retiree who has nothing better to do than complain.

Spoiled Retiree

I had to listen to her whining again. She spoiled my entire day, yet again. Don't get me wrong…I do have compassion for genuine circumstances requiring compassion, kind word or help. This simply wasn't such a situation. While feigning a compassionate tone in affirmative replies, I was grateful that the phone lines didn't transmit the rolling of my eyes.

Again, I am not emotionally frigid. I get it, really. I'm aware that retirees have small pensions, that it's difficult to make ends meet, that all possible health problems attack suddenly and yes, I am aware of the generation gap in understanding notions such as 'compassion', 'help' and 'love'. Besides, those differences in opinion exist even among peers, let alone different generations. But that's not what this is about.

Maybe, it's also a matter of our Central-Eastern European mentality. We need to play the victim, yet none of us can hold our tongues. We love to claim how difficult the circumstances we live in are, yet everyone's away skiing abroad. We hardly make ends meet, yet all the cafés and restaurants are packed. We claim to work like horses, yet no one's ever at work.

I identify this as a matter of our mentality because the previous sentences portray how foreigners see us, especially those from overseas whose list of daily activities drastically differs from our own.

Namely, they don't have notions such as 'social life' or 'vacation'. They wake up every morning at five, only to change from pyjamas into a suit, eat something on the go, buy a coffee to go in a plastic cup, and then spend 2 more hours driving in the morning rush hour to work. Then, they sit in their cubicle offices with their head glued to a computer or work desk from 8 in the morning to 4 in the afternoon and they work as diligently as ants so that their boss wouldn't fire them or put a negative comment on their employment record.

They leave their offices not a minute earlier than 4 in the afternoon, but often much later than that, only to get back into their cars and spend another 2 hours driving home during the afternoon rush hour. By the time they get home, it's already night; they grab a quick bite, change from their suit into their pyjamas and go to bed. They have peace until five in the morning and it all repeats. And that's not only Monday to Friday but Monday to Sunday because many of them simply put—always work.

Here, in our part of Europe? Don't go anywhere on Mondays, all the employees are unpleasant and mad because they had to wake up and get to work; don't go anywhere on Friday, because those that did show up for work on Friday, have already, instantly, left home. A public holiday is on Tuesday? You can forget about getting anything done on the previous Friday, weekend, Monday and of course, the holiday Tuesday.

We are the champions of merging days off. Here, people are always taking some sort of vacation leave, paid one too. As soon as June arrives, the downtowns of most continental cities are stark empty, everyone's on the coast. As soon as December arrives, once more, every city is stark empty, and everyone's off skiing in Austria, Switzerland or Italy. It's embarrassing not to go. What would the neighbours think? And supposedly, there's a horrible recession rummaging around. So they say, but no one's seen it yet though. If this is it, may we always be in a recession!

In the west? The only time people have any break is between 1 and 2 pm when their bosses release them for lunch. In most cases, that's an unpaid lunch break. Then, like ants, they fill up the streets, hurriedly carrying coffee to go in one hand, and in their other hand, either a wrapped hot dog bought at street vendors or a Chinese take-out box. Following trends…what trends? They don't care what colour will be 'in' this fall—they've got much more serious matters on their mind. Mortgages, lines of credit, credit cards, car payments, medical bills, the tax man…

So, when one already has a complete picture of both worlds, verified opinions and experiences that enable a competent comparison of the way of life in the homeland and overseas, it is natural to conclude that the retiree's whining epitomises the spoiled mentality.

Listening to my collocutor complain about the difficult life she's had and all the misfortunes that befell her in the past seventy-something years of her life, my mind recalls a dear, elderly lady I met overseas. A lady in the 7th decade of her life, all by herself…all alone in the world. A lady who in the Balkan war lost the 300 sq. ft. she called home her entire life. A lady who was forced to leave her hometown of Sarajevo in the 6th decade of her life, and to start again, to turn a new leaf in some other city, some other country, other continent, other language area.

She had no choice. Dear, familiar faces of her neighbours were vanishing daily. Some underground, others over the hill to the other side of the trenches. When a grenade destroyed her apartment and she literally lost the roof over her head, what else could she do? Death looked her in the face. Had she remained in her hometown, it would've been a matter of not days but minutes until death came for her. And she wanted to live, to enjoy the beauty of the city whose streets still whispered the secrets of her youth, of her life. Like everyone who genuinely loved that city, the lady too thought, expected, hoped that the war would end soon, that everything would be calm again and that she'd be able to walk by the Miljacka river and relive all those precious moments her hometown had given her.

It was so difficult for her to watch her city suffer, it was so difficult for her to leave it alone, to desert it. But she had to, although she didn't know where she'd go. Or how. With one of the last convoys, she went to Zagreb. She was escorted by the fireworks, the artillery philharmonic orchestra and the glint of the blaze. She left with a tear in her eye, a bundle in her hand and a few Deutsch marks that didn't disappear from the bank, as did her life savings. All she had to take with her were the mental pictures of the life she left behind.

On arrival to Zagreb, she remembered a lady she once knew, with whom she shared a desk in elementary school. That was many, many years ago, but the lady hoped that that old acquaintance would perhaps lend her a hand, give her refuge for a few days at least, only until she could stand on her own feet. Who knew? Maybe the war would end in just a few days. With slow, weary steps, the lady went to the post office, found that old acquaintance's phone number in the phone book and dialled the number.

Although surprised, her old acquaintance was very kind, warm and compassionate. She told the old lady she would send her son to pick her up in a car, and that she would help her in any way she could. That was so nice to hear! Had that acquaintance been different, the old lady would have had to continue turning the pages of her memory, then the pages of the phone book, and who knows how long that would have dragged on or if anyone would have even offered to help her. But she was fortunate with her very first phone call in Zagreb.

She sat on a bench in front of the post office and while waiting for the acquaintance's son to arrive, she observed the people passing by her. They were so calm, slowly walking through the streets, carefree, going after their business. The women were getting out of salons with freshly styled hair and fresh manicures. Others, walking home from the open-air market carrying bags of fresh vegetables and fruits, eggs.

The old lady couldn't exactly recall the last she saw any of those food items, let alone tasted them. Not to mention meat, bread...all food, actually. In her war-torn city, she depended on foreign food aid, but the 'food aid' she received consisted of peanut butter, Tabasco sauce and Yorkshire pudding. That was what they, the foreigners, thought should be given to war-stricken, starved people. And the old lady, like all other prisoners of their love for the occupied city, only wanted bread and water. She only wanted her stomach to stop making sounds, her brain to stop evoking the rich banquettes she used to make for her friends and her own pleasure.

And here, only a few hours away from the hell the old lady left behind, people walked around cheerfully, completely mentally isolated from everything.

They were still making rich banquets, and buying new, trendy clothes; they were laughing, calmly walking in the streets without wondering whether a sniper scope from the surrounding hills is on their forehead. And the old lady felt heartache once again, thinking of the suffering her city was being subjected to. But then, she was also grateful for the detachment of Zagreb, as that gave it the ability to provide her refuge from that suffering.

Her old acquaintance was a widow living in a large apartment and she had enough room to temporarily provide accommodation for the old lady. And so, bit by bit, the old lady started getting used to normal life. She obtained refugee status because she had no other citizenship besides Bosnian, nor could she get any other citizenship. The refugee status enabled her to get healthcare. She was also receiving some financial assistance and food aid. Although she was still living with her acquaintance, she was not a burden in the full sense of the word.

Her daily life normalised but her scars didn't heal. Days and weeks were passing by, months even, and the old lady would still instinctively drop to the ground every time she heard the traditional uptown cannon fire at noon.

Just as the old lady could not get rid of that fear, her old acquaintance also couldn't get rid of the fear that the old lady would never leave. The war everyone expected to end soon was still smouldering without any sign it would soon end, and the old acquaintance had been hearing so many stories about refugees that no one could evict, who occupied apartments under the protected tenant status.

Although the acquaintance had compassion and understanding for the old lady's situation, she also had her own children who were besetting her with horror stories about refugees. Considerately, nicely, but directly, one day the old acquaintance told the old lady she would need to move out as she needed the extra room for her own son and his fiancé who would be moving in with her.

The old lady realised what the problem was…she recognised it in the acquaintance's tone and lowered, embarrassed look, but she didn't take it against her. She was immeasurably grateful to her for her hospitality and utmost kindness. However, the old lady had no money to rent her own apartment, there were even speculations in the news about the abatement of refugee status and assistance, and the war in her hometown was still raging. The only place where the old lady could try to find peace was—overseas. Ironically, the distant continent was her most proximate possibility.

Had she returned to her hometown, even if that were possible, death would certainly await her. And even though she wanted to be buried in her hometown, the sweetest final rest, she wasn't sure that would've been a possibility, she wasn't sure there was any piece of land available for yet another coffin. If she stayed in Zagreb, she'd achieve nothing either, because if she lost her refugee status, that would mean she'd be left to beg in the streets, praying for a piece of bread and some water. No one hires women of her age—they are expected to be retired.

Leaving for another continent, at least she had a hope that she'd welcome death gracefully, with dignity. Perhaps, by that time, the war would end so she could be buried in her homeland. She applied for immigrant status in Canada and was approved.

The old lady packed the bundle she came with to Zagreb, once more, but this time she went to Canada. Fortunately, language was not a problem. She was fluent in English since schooldays, and she knew that communication with others wouldn't be a problem. Since she was already retired and aged, she believed that overseas, in Canada, the social system would take care of her and provide her with dignified last years of her life. She expected no miracles, only a small pension sufficient for life. Even if it's in form of social assistance.

How full of despair she became once she realised that her hope for a decent and dignified remainder of life was nothing but a large Fata Morgana. After the first cultural shock, she realised that overseas, people of her age still worked, sometimes even several jobs at once, just to make ends meet. There was no formulated age of retirement in most cases, a way of life she was used to in her homeland. Overseas, people in the last decades of their lives worked not because they wanted to but because they had to. They were still paying off the mortgages on homes they bought some 30-40 years ago.

On top of that, they had to pay the annual property tax, maintenance fees, utilities, pay healthcare for themselves plus dental separately; they were still paying for public transit at that age, not to mention other required expenses such as annual registration for a car they bought 30 years ago and were still driving. That was the reality…and life called 'the overseas dream' was exactly that—a dream.

This lady knew there was an enormous difference between life overseas and life at home and an even larger difference between her very modest expectations and the reality that awaited her. She thought of the retirement she used to have in her homeland, a truly resting period: in her tiny but very own, mortgage-free apartment, with free medical and dental, free public transit and a pension which, although small, covered all monthly utilities and grocery expenses. With a heavy heart, she recalled her peaceful life, destroyed by war.

And now she found herself in this foreign world, foreign mentality in the 7th decade of her life needing to start from scratch.

The social assistance she was receiving from the government didn't even cover the rent of a studio apartment in the worst part of town. The only option the old lady had was to find a roommate. And unfortunately, there were many people in a similar situation. Thanks to a classified ad in the newspaper, the old lady found a room for rent in a small 2-bedroom apartment. She found a roommate she would split the expenses with—an old Romanian lady.

The lady thought how once upon a peaceful time, she enjoyed her very own 300 sq. ft. of living space, and now in the 7th decade of her life, she had to share that same amount of space with a complete stranger. She had to pay for healthcare and, although it was a large expense, it was an expense that left an impact on her budget, nonetheless. She also had to pay for public transit; she only received a small discount for a monthly pass. In addition, she had to make monthly payments to the government to repay the airplane ticket the government had provided for her arrival to Canada.

Every month, she had to check in with her social worker to explain to him why she still hadn't found a job, why she still didn't get off the social assistance, off the government's back. Useless were her excuses that, in her country, people her age didn't work but enjoyed the retirement instead. The social worker would always tell her that she was now in a new country where people of her age are very vital, full of life and eager to work.

After a few months of adaptation, realising she had no choice, the lady found a job as a building manager of a rental apartment building. The lady was not expected to do any repairs herself, but it was her responsibility to phone the required professional to do necessary repairs such as a leaking pipe, plugged toilet or similar, whomever of the tenants it happened to.

She was though, fully responsible for doing the paperwork for the apartment rentals and keeping the building clean. She was expected to clean the building herself, as her employers couldn't see why a woman of her age wouldn't be able to do so, and the old lady had no desire or strength left to explain or justify a completely different mentality that she was coming from. The plus of this job was that the old lady got a small studio apartment to live in, for a nominal fee. She finally had her peace, although not 'her own' apartment.

But, better something than nothing. Another plus of this situation was that she would finally be receiving slightly more money from this job than she was receiving from social assistance; therefore, she could finally get the disrespectful, bratty social worker off her case and break free from his monthly lectures and questioning.

Every day, the lady was cleaning the washers and dryers in the laundry room shared by all the renters. She cleaned the lobby and the elevator, she vacuumed. Like most average buildings overseas, this one too had an inside pool that the lady had to clean. Every time she looked at that pool, she remembered her first day of work, when the general manager told her that one of the renters using this pool was HIV positive.

He expected the old lady to thoroughly disinfect this pool, to eradicate any possibility of a lawsuit against the building owner. En passant, she was told to make sure she uses thick rubber gloves when disinfecting it. But by that time, nothing could surprise her. She knew how little human life was worth; and how much value was instead put on financial matters. 'To minimise the risk of a lawsuit,' he said… that was the main goal. The lady was not surprised by anything anymore.

By that time, she had gotten used to all kinds of parades she's never seen in her life until then; she became used to seeing a woman sharing the same spoon with her dog, she became used to hearing people talk negatively about babies and children, she became used to seeing people stop and admire a dog passing by while rolling their eyes on hearing a baby cry. She had gotten used to seeing 'No children allowed' signs in cafes and restaurants.

She had gotten used to the fact that no one would get up to give her a seat on the bus just because she was old. She learned that even broth can be bought in a can, as well as mashed potatoes in powder form. She had gotten used to all kinds of street drunks, squatters, and homeless drug addicts, whose scents adorned many sidewalks. She had gotten used to tasteless and scentless fruits and vegetables, on seeing flowers she can't touch, smell or pick, the ocean so dirty and cold no one couldn't swim in.

She had gotten used to mechanised people, immune to family values and anything humane, she had gotten used to the ubiquitous plasticity and replaceability of everything, from a coffee cup to human life. She had gotten used to hypocrisy, shopper mentality and the uncaring attitude towards attire.

Or better said, she learned to embrace all that with respect, as an embodiment of a different culture, but she never assimilated it into her own life. She was here visiting, a guest, a so-called legal alien. The war was still raging, and there was no use to feel pathetic, criticise other cultures or fall into depression. That was it; that was the way her life was meant to be. She had seen everything. There was nothing that could surprise her; could it?

On the day she went to see her GP for the malaise she had been feeling for some time, she did receive one last surprise—they discovered she had metastasised breast cancer. For a moment she was silent, but then she started laughing. Hysterically. That was her destiny, her kismet. It was God's will, it seems, that she was able to get out of the war zone, intact, only to die of breast cancer in the haven of Canada.

This was certainly not the overseas dream she was expecting. It was God's will that she loses the little peace she had and to realise in her final days, how blessed her life was in her homeland. Irony had a completely new meaning. The lady had no money to return to her war-scavenged homeland, and besides, the war was still raging.

'First, they promised to increase the pension by 100 kunas, which itself wouldn't help me at all, but now it turns out they are not increasing but decreasing my pension by that amount!' the voice of spoiled retiree, my co-speaker on the other side of the phone lines, startled me.

'The gas prices went up, and now they want us to pay some extra participation cost when seeing a GP, the prices of fruit and veggies are plain robbery, I can't do all that from my pension! What will I have left to live on until the end of the month? We're old, so we can drop dead for all they care, that's how it works it seems. It's worth nothing to them that we worked all our lives and earned our pensions. And now, what do I do now? I can't cover all the utilities; I have no money left to cover them with!'

'Have you considered selling one of your real estate properties? Maybe you don't really need a paid-off house by the sea and an apartment in the capital city and a weekend getaway in the mountains?' I dared to ask.

'To sell? Oh, no…no, I can't do that…that's all the joy I have left, the fruit of my heavy labour. Real estate is to be kept, not sold! And besides, who'd buy it, people have no money these days!' She fires back.

'It depends on how much you ask. If you ask for a realistic price, you will find a buyer. I mean, it's not like you bought any of those properties with any of your money, you inherited them all either from your husband or your own parents. You never actually had to work to secure yourself a roof over your head, you never had to take out a mortgage loan or any other credit or loan of any kind, ever!' I couldn't hold it back anymore.

'That's all mine!' angrily, she fired back at me. 'I was the one paying utilities for all those properties, and maintaining them…'

'Yes, but if you didn't have money to pay for the utilities, it wouldn't be a tragedy because you do own and possess those properties. No one could kick you out on the street and take the keys. Imagine if you had lost everything or if you had to take loans to buy any of them…'

'If I had lost my properties? Oh, don't you worry, I won't lose anything…it's all mine and mine alone as long as I live.'

'Of course, it is, no will take it away from you, I'm just saying that it's not logical to own 3 mortgage-free prime properties, and whine you've got no money to buy food or pay the utilities. You know what they say, you can't spend the money you don't have. People here are quite spoiled, the only retirees who have any legitimate basis to complain are the ones living overseas, because only they really know what work and difficult life are.

'You know, as an elderly acquaintance of ours said, the only movable he had was his denture and the only immovable he had was in his underwear. What I'm trying to say is, you've got all those real estate properties, movables, immovables, and it's all paid off, I just can't see why you could possibly complain? You can even rent them out to make some money!' I said, quite irritated by this time, thinking how she not only spoiled my entire day but was also going to spoil my entire week.'

'No! No! No! I will not be selling anything! And I don't want some riffraff living in my well-kept houses! I worked hard for it all!' she replies decisively.

Her last sentence caused a sudden burst of laughter out of me, which the retiree on the other side of the telephone line didn't appreciate. I was thinking about the overseas streets which are flooded with people going for a lunch break daily between 1 pm and 2 pm. They rush into the sunshine like ants out of their nests. *They* work! Non-stop. That's work.

Soon, the irritated retiree ended the conversation, which I was very much grateful for. Hanging up, I wondered how much her unjustified whining would cost me this time, but I wouldn't know until the next phone bill. Because, of course, the poor retiree had no money to give *me* a call and I would be marked as a horrible person if I didn't check up on her.

I'm not blaming the retiree for her opinion; she's entitled to it. I'm not blaming anyone. But I am fortunate enough to be familiar with both sides of the coin. The old lady knew that too well. She left her body in a foreign country, but I believe that her soul is hovering in the wind of her hometown of Sarajevo, her homeland. They say, the worst is to have and to lose.

It is the truth. Whoever hasn't lost anything truly valuable, will never understand this. And who has experienced it, understands this too well. The challenge is going back in time, facing your past, facing the ghosts waiting for you. One woman, Stana, did just that. As soon as the war ended, she was able to go back. Reluctantly, but decisively at the same time. She knew she'd have to confront her husband, although he has been dead for years.

Life Unlived

So, she was back. After almost 10 years of exile from her hometown, she was finally back. But it was not a joyful return. It forced her to face the demons she left behind, the memories she wanted to erase, the actions she wanted to deny. But the ghosts of the past all welcomed her back with wide open arms, having been patiently waiting for her all these years.

She didn't go to her husband's grave yet. She wasn't sure what she would say to him. She didn't know if she could even look at his tombstone. She entered their apartment. The same apartment they raised their three children in, the apartment where everything happened—teary laughter, bloody smiles, masked 'all is well' appearances when friends arrived. As soon as she opened the door, she saw a mirrored reflection of herself. She shuddered with embarrassment and anger.

To the left, the kitchen stood still, just as she left it. She glanced at the sink over which she used to stand and do the dishes. For hours, it seemed…sometimes. She walked into the living room slowly, as if not to disturb the ghosts. The old armchair was still under the window; the armchair her husband used to kneel on for hours, just watching the life outside pass him by. She felt the shivers; as if all the demons she left behind in that apartment stood still in front of her, with menacing smiles.

It's funny, her apartment was one of the few that were left intact during the siege, despite the raging battles and horrors around it. She deeply regretted that. She was hoping that one of the grenades would fall right through the window and burn the apartment to the core. She knew, however, that even that wouldn't have destroyed the memories that haunted her.

She walked towards the window and looked outside. The view was very different now. A newly built high-rise right in front of her windows almost entirely blocked the view of the street.

'There'd be nothing for you to watch now,' she said quietly, as if her husband could hear. She looked slightly to the left of the newly built high-rise and saw the cross-shaped intersection. Her lip quivered as her thoughts wandered back to an event 12 years earlier…

'I don't give a damn, you old drunk!' she shouted angrily to her husband who fell on the ground in the middle of the busy intersection. She turned around to leave.

'Where are you going…' her husband was laughing through tears.

He was just sitting there, on the tramlines, like a baby just taught to sit up, with his ruinous cane beside him. It was a Sunday and, luckily, that day the traffic was not busy. However, the tram would arrive, sooner or later. He was physically too weak to get up, and the few extra drinks he's had didn't exactly help. For years, he's had leg muscle atrophy and was walking with the help of a cane. But to get up in this condition, he needed much more help than a cane could provide. And she, his wife, wouldn't help him.

She turned around just long enough to verbally attack him and simply left him sitting on tramlines, instead of giving him support. She didn't even feel any guilt. She was furious. Not only because of his drunken state: it seemed she was furious from the day they got married. She was furious that he worked all the time, sometimes even three different jobs at a time. She was furious that she spent her life at home, raising children.

She was furious because all those years she felt neglected, invisible. She was furious because her youth flew by and she never got to live through it. She was furious that her life was passing by rapidly, and she couldn't hold onto it. She was furious because she couldn't return the time and she never got to do so many things, to see so many places, to experience everything that life has to offer.

He never wanted to take her anywhere, he was always working. Or always tired. Or simply not wanting to go anywhere.

She got married when she was only 18 years old and had dedicated her whole life to him and their children. And whoever dedicated anything to her?

She despised him and blamed him for all of her own defaults and weaknesses. She didn't have enough strength, enough willpower to do something, to make changes…or to simply leave. Frustrations grew from day to day and accumulated over the years.

Having left him sitting on the ground, she returned to their apartment without any remorse and went straight to the kitchen to do the dishes. She didn't even peek through the window to see whether her husband was still sitting on the tramlines, whether he was still alive.

'You old fool, what were you thinking?' She heard the angry, panic-stricken voice of their son who was hurriedly rushing out of the apartment, in an undershirt and sweatpants.

She just continued doing the dishes, as if nothing had happened.

She was thinking about numbers…number 40, the number of years she spent in this marriage, the years of her precious life she simply threw in the wind, the years she disowned too easily, years of life she took for granted.

She used to love writing poems; she could've been a famous poetess. She used to love to sew and knit; she could've been the Coco Chanel of the Balkans. She could've been so many things, but now…Here she was, nearing the age of 60, with three grown children, at the brink of her life. And she was wondering, where did her youth disappear to?

She was furious. What she forgot though, is that she gave birth to those children in order to bind him. She also forgot that all those years she had intentionally been suppressing her own dreams. Because she knew, if she left him, he'd remarry fast.

He was a good catch: tall, dark, handsome, highly educated, ambitious, esteemed—all women would wish him for a husband. And then what would she do, be a single mother with three children? In that age and time, that social environment?

This way, at least she had all those damn fur coats, all that damn jewellery. Regardless, he *was* to blame. It was all his fault. He was to blame because he was so damn passive.

She remembered one specific evening, a dance night at a local community centre. She bought herself a new dress and spent eternity on her make-up. She put on his favourite perfume, kids were put to bed, and she waited for him to come home and take her dancing. He said he would. She was so excited! It has been such a long time since she danced! She patiently waited, all dressed up. Finally, he came home and went straight to bed. He went to sleep! After all her effort, all the energy she put in to make herself look so pretty for him, wanting them to go out somewhere, to have a nice time… he just went to sleep. This dance was the highlight she was looking forward to, for months! She was all dressed up and had nowhere to go.

Yes, he was tired because that day he worked all three jobs consecutively, but that was irrelevant to her. He always worked. That should've been her evening…and he ruined it…just like he ruined every other evening.

With time, he spent more and more time away from home. First, it was for work but then, when he retired, he was simply running away from home. From her. He went to the park, to a bar, anywhere but home. She found her consolation in others…she had to. She needed to feel desirable, loved, wanted …even just for an hour, even if just for pretend. She tried talking to him about her feelings many, many, many times. But he was too busy.

Her frustrations turned into rage, and it just grew. First, she'd throw nasty words at him, and then, those words turned into crystal vases, ashtrays, anything at hand. However, no matter how much she insulted or hit him, sometimes until he bled, he never reacted the way she wanted him to. He never defended himself in any way…he just looked her straight in the eyes and laughed through bloody tears. That made her furious…his laugh irritated her even more. So damn passive…

And then she found herself here, alone in the kitchen, nervously doing the dishes, not thinking about how she left her husband in the middle of the tramlines. For the first time in her life, she didn't care about what the neighbours thought.

'You old fool! Don't you even think about laying a hand on him ever again!' she heard her son's threatening voice, and the drunken, soft laughter of her husband. She didn't even turn around. She knew he'd still have that stupid teary smile on his face.

'He could've been run over by a tram…or a car!' the son continued, helping his father sit down on a chair. 'Just leave him alone…You should be ashamed of yourself; poor man has slaved off his entire life for you and your fucking fur coats!' the son shouted.

The husband was just sitting on a kitchen chair, smiling through tears. Like a baby placed in a highchair. She didn't even look at him, she just continued doing the dishes. But she knew…she knew that he was sitting with his legs crossed, one elbow on the table, the other on the armrest of the chair. She knew already…he was sitting there and snorting with that stupid face.

She knew…she knew what she'd see if she were to look at him, but she didn't know what she wouldn't have seen if she had looked at him. She wouldn't have known that there sat a man who learned to laugh at all the misery life brought him. She wouldn't have known that there sat a man who had embarked on a path of no return. She wouldn't have known that there sat a man with a deep secret, a man who knew he had but a few moments left in this miserable life of his.

A few years after the tramline incident, he suddenly died of metastasised cancer, shocking everyone in the family. The fact is, he knew he was ill for years before but didn't tell anyone, not even his children. He decided to leave that life…he had no desire to fight for it. And why would he?

Now, at the age of 80, she sat in the same chair he used to sit in all those years ago, but now she was all alone and seeing things from his perspective. He never raised his voice or hand at her, but he did give her one blow that caused a scar that would never heal—he chose death over the fight for life with her.

Going back to the memories, to the homeland, after the war ended, felt strange for every one of us. We felt tingling…there were tears, a feeling of restlessness. Joy and sadness. Fear. Even if going just for a visit, knowing I'd be walking those streets again, including the street in the city centre, where a grenade tore tens of people's limbs at the very beginning of the war. My cousin was one of them.

The holes grenade explosion made on the sidewalk were filled with red cement… as an eternal testament of what happened…our very own 'Je me souviens'…our very own 'N'oubliez pas'.

The pigeons didn't coo the same way, the church bells didn't toll the same way, the mosque's imam didn't sing the same way, and the synagogue's service didn't feel the same way. Nothing seemed the same, yet the scents were all the same. We'd close our eyes and see everything as it was—childhood, life before the war, happiness, laughter. Small things, you know? Small, but happy things.

However, for a woman from Srebrenica, that was not the case. She could never decide what was worse, having her eyes closed or open, because she wasn't killed or raped 'just' once or twice. She was being continuously raped again, and again by them, and by him.

Srebrenica

There he was, standing only a few metres away from her at their local grocery store. She almost dropped her bag from the shock. He too, first gave her a startled, guilty look that then turned into a smirk: a malicious, satisfied smirk. And He could afford to behave that way. He was released from any charges as he was 'too small' of a fish… He only worked *'under command of his superior'*, they said. *Not guilty. He did what he was told to do.* They released him, and he came back to continue living in the same town, to walk the same streets, to shop at the same grocery store as She did. The law couldn't touch him; it was his hometown as well. He was as protected as an endangered animal.

Before it became his hometown, it was hers. Small and peaceful, but lovingly hers, nonetheless. No 'big' events happened there, aside from a local cow giving birth or the peak of excitement—someone getting married. She lived there a peaceful life, with her new husband, her parents, her siblings, and their families. She was expecting her first child with her husband—a baby boy, they were told—and she was about 7 months pregnant at the time. The time of what? The time of eradication. Ethnic cleansing.

That was the time when a few other people, living in the same town, started being bothered by the people of 'her' kind—people belonging to a different religion. It would have been something as relatively minor as drunken, unintentional words of discrimination, had not those people been supported by an entire army of the same thinkers. Literally—an army. So, with their help, one day they decided to start the eradication of 'her kind' from that town. Suddenly, they saw people of her religion as a disease, plaguing over what they considered to be *their* city.

Despite the fact that no one bothered anyone, despite the fact they were all mostly non-practising in their respective religions, despite the fact it was wrong to kill others based on their religion—to say the least. Despite all sense and reason. They just wanted to make it 'ethnically pure'.

It was done fairly fast, the brutal eradication. Men were tortured in the most unthinkable ways and killed in even more unthinkable ways. Women and female children were raped in the most unfathomable ways and kept aside for further use in other unfathomable ways. Just because. But for her, he had a special plan. He was now one of those soldiers in power. He could go through with anything he wanted; with the sick plan he's been creating in his mind for years…a plan that would put Marquis de Sade's 'creativity' to shame.

The soldier always had his eyes on her. She knew this for many years but didn't share the feeling; she considered him a friend. She always exchanged a few words with him casually on the street and she always said hi to him. She did it a little out of guilt she didn't reciprocate his feelings but mostly out of the kindness she displayed towards all her neighbours.

Such is life, she thought. You can't choose who you fall in love with, so she could at least be kind to him.

She knew he was hurt when she got married and when she was walking around with her love child in the tummy. She also naively believed that he would be happy for her if he did indeed love her. That he would be happy simply because she was happy. She had no idea, she never could have imagined it; to this day, she couldn't fathom that he'd be capable of hurting her so much, in such a tyrannical way, mildly put.

Because when the eradication time had come, all of the unwanted, 'impure' inhabitants were completely taken by surprise. It was easy to eradicate them, they had nothing to defend themselves with, and they were in a friendly state of mind with no clue as to the possibility of something as dreadful as the atrocious plan these soldiers had in mind. Her husband, her father, her brother and his son were all taken away one morning. She never saw them again.

Technically speaking, she did see the bones and skull of her father many, many, many years later. She couldn't identify him obviously, but the foreign workers told her it was her father…DNA matched. As for her husband, brother and his son, they were never found. She was far from being the only female in town with this story. All other men in the families like hers were met with the same destiny, if one can call this intentional act of eradication— 'destiny'.

Women were also taken away; the houses were burned. It is completely redundant to detail or even mention the actions women were subjected to. All the possible negative scenarios you can think of—you will be right.

But what the soldier had in mind for Her, was the peak of the darkness of the human mind. The peak.

When she saw him approach her in the concentration camp she was taken to, she was glad. She saw one friendly face on the other side of the reason, one good heart in the wolf uniform and she hoped he'd be her Schindler, her Rolf in a more atrocious version of the script, perhaps 'the Sounds of Pain'.

He came up to her and told her that he'd take her away from the concentration camp and release her in the nearby forest, from where she could get to foreign aid workers and save herself. She was so grateful to him for those words, for the promised help. At the same time, she was ashamed that she should be saved when so many others would die. Ashamed that she should hope to be saved when she didn't even know where her husband was or whether he was alive. But she had a baby in her tummy she had to think of. She had no choice.

Soon, she found herself on the other side of the fence. She was free—or so she thought. He walked in front of her, staying quiet but taking determined steps toward the forest. She walked behind him as fast as she could, holding one hand on her tummy, gently rubbing it. They were already deep in the forest when he stopped walking and turned back towards her without saying anything. She smiled uneasily. She had a bad premonition. And she was right.

He came towards her and pushed her to the ground. She fell on her back, screaming and asking him what he was doing. He replied that he waited for that day all of his life, patiently waiting to have her. He said it was a 'pity' he had to have her this way, in her condition, but he was so glad to finally have her. And no one could prevent him. No one.

As he was saying that and unbuttoning his pants, she was screaming and crying, trying to crawl away from him, as much as her large tummy allowed her to. She knew she could not escape him. She continued screaming as he came on top of her, she sobbed as he violated her, and she yelled in pain thinking of the baby in her tummy…but to no avail. She knew that. She felt helpless, she could not breathe…she felt like she fell deep into a cave she couldn't get out of. Like she was sinking into quicksand. She had no way out. She could get no help. At some point, she stopped. She just lay there like a tree, with tears silently escaping the corners of her eyes. She just stared at the sky. Numb. Completely numb.

When he was done, he got up and buttoned up. But he wasn't done. Talking about a bastard child of the damned religion—the baby in her tummy, he took out his army knife and performed a C section on her, mildly put. Right then and there. Just because. She was already half-dead out of pain, blood loss and shock, mostly unconscious when she vaguely heard the only cry her baby let out, just before the soldier killed him. She could only softly, weakly whisper 'my baby'…and let out one single bloody tear. The soldier put the baby's body in front of her eyes.

'There's your bastard,' he said. 'But don't worry, you'll join him soon,' he added. He spat on her, then left. Leaving her to bleed out. Leaving her to die.

But she didn't. She never remembered what happened after that, as she lost consciousness. When she woke up again, she was in the foreign aid workers' care, in a place that looked a little like a hospital room and a little like an office.

'She's back! She's conscious!' someone screamed.

'Baby...' she said quietly, tears softly falling down her face. She knew there was no baby anymore. She knew, but she couldn't cope with it.

'It's ok...' a nurse said to her in a soft, breaking voice, and gently stroked her hair.

Five years had passed since then. She was eternally scarred, but alive. Her only goal, the reason that kept her going was to see justice served. To find out her husband's and baby's resting places, to see the judicial system punish the soldier for his monstrosity, to regain bits and pieces of what was left of her life, to get through each day. But none of it happened. Years passed by; she never found out where her husband's remains were located, nor those of her baby.

Despite the ordeal she herself had gone through; her soul always burned more when thinking of the death her husband must have met. She loved him so much. But she never found him again. The judicial system released the soldier, claiming he did as he was told and that he was at no fault at all.

Besides, there were no other witnesses so, to them, it was as simple as her word against his. As if she would do all that to herself! As if she could! That outcome was not only a psychological rape of her, but an approval of the violation and monstrosity she's been through.

There was never any closure on anything. She just couldn't regain control of her life. She tried so hard, but she couldn't get it together. She wanted to; she really did. She tried to. Every day, every hour, every minute. She tried to find something positive, to discover some purpose, to uncover something beautiful and encouraging around her, to give her strength to go on. But seeing his smirk today... was like being pushed down from the mountain cliff she worked so hard to climb up. That smirk of his… it was like kicking someone who's already down.

That same week, they found her lifeless body at her home. She overdosed on sedatives. There was no message, no mess…she was lying in her bed, pale and tranquil, firmly grasping in her left fist the only evidence of the only nice memory she had left—her wedding ring. Her right hand was resting on her scarred tummy. *If they couldn't have their happily after on Earth, they would live happily ever after in heaven. In heaven, they will find peace and family joy, and will surely live as the most blessed and happiest of all.* Those were her last thoughts. She escaped Earthly reality in the hope the Heavenly one would be better.

There are many kinds of escapes from reality. When things were hard, I remember thinking that perhaps it wasn't Canada to blame, that perhaps it was the city. That it was us. But it's easier to change the city, than ourselves. So, we moved to the East Coast, anticipating things would be better, more like what we had back home…more similar mentality, architecture, and values. It was not the answer. So, we decided to change the surroundings yet again, but God wouldn't let me leave before I made the change within myself first.

Side by a Hasid

I'm not an anti-Semite, that's a fact. But when I moved to a Montreal neighbourhood largely inhabited by Hasidic Jews, I cannot say I felt indifferent. Born and raised in Sarajevo, in a multireligious family, I was brought up with enormous respect, acceptance and openness toward any religion. Still, living among ghostly pale people all dressed in black with floor-length black coats, tall black hats and braided sideburns, instilled some fear in me. However, a 7-hour plane ride forced me to face my fear and completely dissolved all my misconceptions about Hasidic Jews.

Because a Hasidic Jew took a plane seat right next to me.

Moving to Montreal, my husband and I knew very little of the city, so we did a quick online search that briefly acquainted us with various neighbourhoods. The neighbourhood of Côte St-Luc constantly popped out as a family-friendly, low-traffic, English-speaking area mostly inhabited by the Jews. We found an apartment online, and a few months later, we were residents of Montreal!

When the online search talked about Jewish population living in Côte St Luc, I didn't have a clue they were talking about *these* Jews, the Hasidic Jews. Even if they did mention the Hasidic Jews, I wouldn't have understood much about what it meant. It was enough for me to look at them, and I felt fear and a strong urge to run in the opposite direction, almost like a hunted animal.

Occasionally, I almost did feel that way, not as a hunted animal, but as an endangered species in that neighbourhood. It felt as if I were the only female wearing make-up, heels and pants. My apartment windows were the only lit ones, while everyone else's was starkly dark, as they celebrated Tisha B'Av. My window was the only one with the Christmas tree silhouette, while all the other ones had menorahs. I embraced the differences, but I did secretly fear that *I* bothered *them*. After all, my family and I were the ones standing out.

None of my neighbours ever said anything to me throughout my residence in that area. And maybe that was the problem, as all I thought I knew about them, I found out online. They were portrayed as people living in the old ages, ignorant of any modern media such as computers and cell phones, mostly eating raw fruits and vegetables, unsocial even among themselves. Ironically, all the time I was living in that area, one of the safest areas of Montreal, I felt unsafe.

Being a hybrid of multiple religions, I was not raised to disrespect anyone or fear anything different. But this was stronger than me, and only when we decided to move out of the area, did I feel relief. However, it was far from over; God was apparently displeased with my feelings and had decided to teach me a lesson.

When my daughter and I took aisle seats on a plane bound for Frankfurt, I was shocked to see a Hasidic Jew matching the seat number on his plane ticket to a seat number right next to me. '*You've got to be kidding,*' I thought to myself. This plane had over 300 seats, and of all of these seats, a Hasidic

Jew had a seat right next to me. So, there was me in the middle, my young daughter to my right and a Hasidic Jew to my left.

At first, I felt discomfort, but then I thought it was a hilarious Deus ex machina. Nevertheless, I kept my head turned towards my daughter, afraid of turning my head in his direction. I remember thinking how that would be the longest flight ever.

I was carefully choosing which movies to watch, as my TV screen was visible to the seat right next to me. I knew that it was not the time to watch Baywatch—not that I was planning on it! I tried to be as quiet and invisible as possible and tried to keep my daughter quiet as well.

Then, out of the blue, the Hasidic Jew sitting next to me took a laptop out of his travel bag, opened it, lightly touched my arm and pointed his finger toward his monitor background while giving me a discreet, friendly smile. I looked at his laptop and saw a photo of two beautiful little girls, about the same age as my own daughter, sitting under a tree in a park and happily smiling. They wore long pink dresses and had neatly tied ponytails.

'These are my daughters,' he said to me. For a moment I was speechless. I am unsure whether I was more shocked by the fact that he had a laptop, that he was speaking to me or that he appeared to be a very normal person, a proud father of two beautiful little girls. Slowly, I started speaking too, and by the end of the flight, all of my misconceptions were broken.

It is strange that it only took a few hours for a 3-year-long fear of the unknown to disappear. I realised that the Hasidic Jews were not perhaps actually unsocial but rather perceived as such. Perhaps it was because they are protective of their religious values and because they are aware of the misconceptions about them. Instead of spending hours reading about them and being fearful, all I should have done is—asked.

Suddenly the 3-year period spent living in that area didn't seem so dark, looking at it in retrospect. And while I was initially upset that God gave me this crash-course on review of my values, I am glad I got the chance to not only face my fear, but also gain a new acquaintance.

It seems, no matter what change life brings upon us, no matter how horrible, unexpected, fearful, or unfair it is—only the change within ourselves is what will make us or break us.

As for me, I am ashamed to say I haven't been back to my homeland in over 20 years. That one time I did go, after the war ended, the scars were still fresh…and painful. Twenty years later, I was not sure I've healed enough to go back. I couldn't just go back superficially, visit friends, eat traditional food and go sightseeing.

For me, every face and every building, or worse—the lack of a face, or a building, would make me restless. I felt the void by not going back, but you can't fill the void with emptiness, can you? I respect my home, my birth city…it stands strong after all it has endured, but like accomplices who suffered the same pain, for over 20 years I felt we weren't ready to face each other yet. But I did go, I faced my own ghosts, memories, remnants of a life I used to lead…I don't remember ever crying that much like during that visit to my birth city.

I never cry, you know. Never, for anything meaningful. Never since the day I left my beloved, besieged city of Sarajevo. I keep it bottled and carry on. From day to day, from year to year. Carrying on is my purgatory, speaking about it is my therapy. And this was my story and the story of the rest of us, people you don't want to meet, with stories you don't want to read about. And there are so many more that remain untold…